Keep it Clean

ob

yn Dinan

— Contents —

LONGMAN

—Chapter 1—

"Our Environment"

It was the first day back at school after the Easter holidays and Samuel Simpson was not in a good mood. The morning had gone smoothly enough and it was not that Sam didn't get on with Mrs Wilson, the class teacher. No, it was just that Easter had been such a good break and Sam did not feel like returning to work. His sister Kerry was a year younger and she couldn't wait to get back – but Sam was in a bad mood and everyone knew it.

"Why are you in such a bad mood?" whispered Tiger. (His real name was Tahir but as he often wore bright, stripy jumpers, he was usually referred to as Tiger – which made him feel very important.) "What's the matter with you?"

"I'm not in a bad mood, " growled Sam. "It's just that everyone else is so cheerful. I don't understand why everyone's so cheerful about coming back to school!"

Tiger nudged Sam with his elbow and said, "Did you get many Easter eggs? I only got three and Scratch ate one of them."

Scratch was Tiger's dog – the most strange, lop-sided mongrel imaginable.

"I don't think he meant to eat it," continued Tiger. "It fell off the kitchen table and he sort of – tidied it up. He's thoughtful like that."

Sam scowled and looked the other way.

"I bought Scratch an Easter present, " persisted Tiger. "I bought him a new collar from the supermarket. It was in the sale. It's not everyone's cup of tea but Scratch likes it."

Sam sighed and shook his head.

"Now then," said Mrs Wilson from the front of the class. "It's time we made a start. This afternoon we are going to begin our new topic, which is 'Our Environment'."

Tiger grinned and looked interested.

"I like topic work," he whispered. "It's good fun!"

"I think we'd all agree that we want to do whatever is possible to avoid litter and pollution in our environment. The question is, where do we start?" Mrs Wilson paused and looked at the children staring back at her. "Any ideas?"

Lucy Hollins put her hand up and said,

"My mum thinks everyone should vote for Mr Crompton in the local elections. He's against litter and pollution. He really cares. All his posters say so."

Mrs Wilson coughed and looked uncomfortable.

"Thank you, Lucy, but I don't think we should bring politics into our topic work, do you? What do you think we could do ourselves to improve the environment?"

Tiger's hand shot into the air and he waved it about frantically. Mrs Wilson nodded at him.

"We could design our own posters, Mrs Wilson, telling people not to drop litter or pollute the town."

"Excellent idea, Tahir," said Mrs Wilson and she

rubbed her hands with pleasure.

"We'll definitely design our own posters and we'll display them around the school. We could even ask some of the local shops if they would put up a poster in their window. What else could we do?"

"We could make slogans for our posters," said Tiger. "It would help people remember them."

"Yes, we'll come back to the posters ," said Mrs Wilson. "Other ideas, please?"

Richard Hooper had a suggestion.

"Why don't we start by finishing our new conservation area? Mrs Lewis' class have made the pond but the rest of the area needs clearing up."

Mrs Wilson's eyes lit up.

"Ah!" she said. "What a very good practical idea, Richard."

She stood up and paced backwards and forwards.

"It just so happens that the Blackshaw Building Society is sponsoring a 'Keep It Clean' campaign. If we agree to take part in the campaign, the building society will supply a 'Keep It Clean' kit – black polythene bags, plastic gloves – the lot. What do you say? Shall we give it a go?"

The class's response was positive and enthusiastic. Even Sam had become involved and he nodded his agreement with the rest of the children. Only Tiger looked thoughtful. He rubbed his nose, scratched his head and then suddenly shot his hand up again and said,

"I think I've got my slogan, Miss!" He pulled himself to his feet and said in a loud voice, "Get rid of unsightly litter, try to make our town much fitter!"

The class roared with laughter as Mrs Wilson shook her head in dismay.

Ten minutes later, Mrs Wilson and her class were gathered together in the conservation area. It was really no more than a piece of waste ground behind the school, which the children had started to clear and use as a science resource. Kerry had already explained to Sam and Tiger how her class had designed and built a pond.

"We're putting goldfish in the pond," Kerry had explained. "We've got some in our classroom at the moment. One of them's huge. Mrs Lewis has had him for years."

As the children clustered around Mrs Wilson, they could see Mrs Lewis' class near their pond. Sam waved to his sister and then pushed forward next to Tiger. It was a fine, spring day. The sun was shining and they were out of the classroom. Yes, Sam was definitely in a better mood.

"Right," said Mrs Wilson, using her favourite word to attract attention. "Plenty of planting to do this afternoon. We've got a dozen young saplings to plant and several shrubs – cuttings from my garden I'm proud to say. We'll dig the holes and put some compost in the bottom. Our compost heap has been a great success; it's produced some lovely, steaming compost! Remember, when you've finished planting, firm the ground around the base with your feet. Now, I've marked the planting areas. Get yourselves into twos and off you go."

The class dispersed and the next half hour saw a flurry of activity in the conservation area. The children became totally absorbed in their tasks and Mrs Wilson flitted around like a spring fly, delighted that her lesson was being received so well.

Tiger and Sam were working together near the high exterior wall. They had planted a sapling and were carefully attaching a support to a wooden stake when three leering faces appeared above the wall.

"What are you up to?" said the middle face.

Tiger recognised the voice immediately and a quick glance at the spotty face confirmed that it was Vetch, a particularly nasty older boy. The girl on his left was Karen Cooper, known as 'Kaz' to her friends. She was chewing gum and twisting a strand of lank, brown hair around her finger. Neither Sam nor Tiger recognised the face of the boy on the right. He had short-cropped, ginger hair that seemed to stand straight up on top of his head.

The ginger-haired boy scratched his head and said,

"Yeah, what are you doing?"

"I'm planting a tree, " said Tiger in disgust. "What does it look like I'm doing?"

"Why are you planting a tree there?" said Vetch. "What's the point of putting a tree there?"

"Because it will look nice, " said Tiger. "Trees look nice. That's why we're planting them."

"That's stupid," hissed Vetch. "You won't get trees to grow there. They'll die."

"No they won't," said Sam. "This is a conservation area. We've built a pond and now we're planting trees and shrubs. If they're looked after properly, there's no reason why they should die."

"I'm telling you they're going to die," said Vetch and his two friends nodded in agreement. "And if you don't believe me, wait and see."

The argument was interrupted by a new sound, a familiar rasping noise that made Tiger glance from side to side in anticipation.

"That's Scratch," he said. "I'd know his bark anywhere. I wonder where he is?"

Tiger's question was answered the very next moment as a small, brown-haired mongrel sauntered through the school gate, barking into the air every so often, long tail wafting backwards and forwards.

"What's that?" roared Vetch. He pointed at the dog and bellowed with laughter. "What is that animal?"

"That's Scratch," said Tiger, seriously. "And I'll have you know he's a very clever dog."

"Clever! That?" said Vetch. He was hardly able to contain himself. "And what's that yellow thing he's got round his neck?"

"That's Scratch's new collar," said Tiger, slowly and deliberately, his face turning red with anger. "If you must know, I bought it for him for Easter."

Scratch chose that very moment to saunter up to Tiger and, as he approached, a faint tinkling sound could be heard. Before he reached the boys, the dog stopped and scratched at his collar with one of his back legs.

Sam nudged Tiger with his elbow and said in a hoarse whisper, "Tiger – it's a cat's collar. It's got a bell on it, Tiger! You've gone and bought him a cat's collar!"

Tiger looked surprised and said, "I know that, Sam. It was a bit cheaper, you see. Besides, Scratch can't tell the difference, can he?"

"It's a cat's collar!" roared Vetch. "Did you hear that, Ginger? That stupid animal's wearing a cat's collar with a bell on it! No wonder it looks confused!"

"Yeah, stupid!" replied Ginger.

Kaz spat out her chewing gum and said, "It's like this whole project – stupid! You'll never get this dump of an area looking nice. You're wasting your time if you ask me."

"Now then," said Mrs Wilson, approaching briskly. "We have no time to waste this afternoon, Tahir and Sam. You'll have to arrange to talk to your friends after school."

Vetch and his two companions dropped down behind the wall and, as they walked away, they could be heard mimicking the teacher's voice. Mrs Wilson frowned and turned her attention to Scratch, who was in the middle of another bout of scratching.

"It's not good enough, Tahir," said the teacher. "It's irresponsible to allow your pet to wander the streets freely. What if he caused an accident? How would you feel then? It is quite clear that if a dog is to be allowed out it should be kept on a lead."

"I'm sorry," said Tiger, taking hold of Scratch by his new collar. "He must have got out of the back yard."

"Well, you'd better take him home," said Mrs Wilson. "Make sure you come straight back, mind. School doesn't finish for another forty-five minutes and I'll want some volunteers to collect our 'Keep It Clean' kit from the Blackshaw Building Society."

"Thank you," said Tiger, dragging Scratch towards the gate. "Thank you very much. And I'll be one of your volunteers, Miss. I'm very keen to keep it clean!" He stopped and stood up straight. "That's even better than my first slogan – 'I'm very keen to keep it clean!' "

Mrs Wilson raised her hands to her eyes and shook her head as Scratch broke free from Tiger's grip and ran out of the school gate, barking loudly.

—Chapter 2—
The witness

At four o'clock that same afternoon, Tiger took it upon himself to visit the Blackshaw Building Society to collect a 'Keep It Clean' kit for the school project. The building society was at the far end of High Street and, as Tiger made his way along, he held on to an old leather lead attached to a subdued-looking Scratch who was trotting dejectedly by his side.

"It's no use you sulking, Scratch," said Tiger, firmly. "Mrs Wilson's quite right. Blackshaw is a busy, built-up area and you should be kept on a lead."

It was about a twenty-minute walk from Tiger's house to the far end of High Street and Tiger wanted to make sure he arrived at the building society before it closed at four-thirty. He left the open market, cut along Brook Street and came out into High Street almost opposite the building society.

"Well, look at that!" he said as he stood at the kerbside waiting to cross the busy main road. "There's a car parked on the double yellow lines right in front of the building society. That's what I call lazy, Scratch. There's a car park just around the corner."

Sure enough, a large maroon hatchback had stopped directly opposite the double doors of the Blackshaw Building Society and, as Tiger watched, the driver's window was lowered and an empty cigarette packet was tossed out on to the road.

"I don't believe it!" said Tiger. "Did you see that, Scratch? There's a huge poster in the window advertising the 'Keep It Clean' campaign and the driver of that car just chucks his rubbish on to the road! I'm going to say something!"

Tiger approached the car, peered in through the tinted window that had been wound back up and rapped loudly on the glass. There was no response whatsoever.

Tiger glanced down and said, "I'm getting annoyed, Scratch. I'm getting very annoyed!"

He knocked again, longer and louder, and then he took a step back as the window slid down until it was about half open. Tiger could just make out a slim figure dressed in dark clothing, the face partly concealed by a khaki army hat and dark glasses. Tiger could not be sure but he had the feeling it was a woman driver.

"What's the problem, kid?" It was definitely a woman. The voice was high-pitched and very irritable.

"The problem," said Tiger, slowly and deliberately, "is litter! You're parked on double yellow lines right outside the Blackshaw Building Society which is sponsoring a 'Keep It Clean' campaign and you throw litter out of your window. What do you say to that?"

There was no time for the driver to answer for, at that moment, the late-afternoon peace was shattered by a piercing alarm bell. The car window shot up and the engine roared into life. Almost immediately, the double

doors of the building society burst apart and two masked
figures raced towards the car. One of the figures barged
into Tiger and sent him sprawling across the pavement,
his head crashing against the open door of the building
society.

Scratch's tail shot in between his hind-legs and he ran
off up the road as fast as he could, the tattered leather
lead trailing behind him.

The car was already moving forward as the men
pulled the back door open, tossed two canvas bags in
ahead of them and then tumbled inside themselves.

The whole incident had taken a matter of seconds
and, as Tiger stumbled to his feet, he was stunned and
deeply shocked.

Some fifteen minutes later, Tiger was sitting in the manager's office of the Blackshaw Building Society, an ice pack held against his bruised and aching head. A police officer approached the boy, notebook in hand.

"Now then," he said. "My name is Inspector Fairhurst. Perhaps you'd like to tell me all that you saw – if you're feeling up to it, that is?"

"I'm all right," said Tiger. "Bit of a headache, that's all. I just can't believe it. I'd only come for a 'Keep It Clean' kit!"

"Let's start from the beginning, shall we?" said the officer, smiling. "Give me your name and address and we'll take it from there."

"Well, it all started with Scratch coming to school ..." began Tiger, and he went on to relate the whole story, finishing with the words, "I just can't believe it! I'd only come to collect a 'Keep It Clean' kit!"

"That's great," said Inspector Fairhurst, closing his notebook. "I only wish all our witnesses were as reliable as you. And you suspect the getaway driver could have been a woman? That really is very interesting."

"It was the voice you see," said Tiger. "I'm sure it was a woman's voice."

"We have another eye witness who may be able to confirm that," said Inspector Fairhurst. "The maroon getaway car was seen swerving across the road about half a mile from the scene of the robbery. Apparently, the driver swerved to miss some stupid dog that ran into the road trailing a lead behind it. The car narrowly missed a lamp post and our witness was able to get a good look at the driver."

"That sounds like Scratch," said Tiger, indignantly. "I'll have you know that's my dog and he's not at all stupid. In fact, when he realised there was a robbery going on, he gave chase. That's probably why he was half a mile from the scene. That's probably why he caused the car to swerve."

The inspector coughed uncomfortably.

"Er … yes," he said. "Well, you'll be pleased to know that the animal is safe. My constable will take a few more details from you and then we'll get you home. And don't forget. If you remember anything else about the robbery, you ring Blackshaw Police Station and ask for Inspector Fairhurst."

"Thank you very much," said Tiger, standing up. "But I can tell you now – I'm not going home without my 'Keep It Clean' kit!"

Later that evening, Tiger went round to Sam's house. He rapped loudly on the front door and, when Kerry opened it, he stepped inside and said, "You'll never guess what happened to me earlier on!"

"You saw a robbery," said Kerry, pulling a face as she caught sight of Tiger's yellow and black striped jumper. "You went to the building society and you saw a robbery take place."

Tiger was astounded.

"How did you know that?" he stammered. "It only happened a couple of hours ago!"

"News travels quickly," said Kerry. "Come on through and tell us all about it."

Tiger followed Kerry along the short hallway and into the kitchen where Mr and Mrs Simpson were sitting on either side of a small table. Mrs Simpson was clutching a mug of hot tea and she pushed another one towards her husband as Tiger entered.

Mr Simpson looked up from his newspaper and said,

"Believe you've got yourself in a bit of bother, lad?"

"It's not like that, Father," said Mrs Simpson quickly. "Tahir just happened to witness a robbery. He can't be blamed for that, can he?"

Mr Simpson sipped his tea and buried his head in his paper.

At that moment, Sam came downstairs and said,

"Hello, Tiger! What's this about a robbery, then?"

"Let's go out for a walk," said Tiger, "and I'll tell you all about it."

Five minutes later, the children were walking along a rough footpath that led down to Blackshaw River. Tiger often went down to the river to do a bit of fishing. Scratch was with them and, once they had reached the footpath, the dog was let off his lead and allowed to roam freely. It was a lovely, clear, spring evening and, although the sun was setting, there would be a good hour before it grew dark.

Tiger told Sam and Kerry the whole story. He exaggerated a little, particularly with regard to Scratch's bravery, but nevertheless, Sam and Kerry were very impressed.

When the children got to the river, they scrambled up a steep track and stood on an old stone bridge overlooking the water. One lone fisherman sat on the bank a few hundred metres away, his rod motionless over the still evening water.

"I even remembered to pick up a 'Keep It Clean' kit," said Tiger, proudly. "That's what I went for, you see."

"We could do with that around here," said Kerry. "There's rubbish everywhere. In fact, it's like a tip."

Kerry was right. From their vantage point on the bridge, the children could see an assortment of empty tin cans, old newspapers and cardboard packages littering the sides of the river and the surrounding area. Worse still, larger items, which had been discarded by lazy householders, had been dumped and left to rot into the landscape.

"Another thing," said Kerry, sniffing the air. "It's smelly. There's a funny smell around here."

"I noticed that," said Sam, "but I didn't like saying anything. I thought it was Tiger's feet!"

"Of course it's not my feet," said Tiger, indignantly. "But yes, there is a strange smell. It's not been here before."

"It's like bad eggs," said Kerry, screwing up her face. "Don't let's stay here too long."

"No, it's more like bad fish," said Sam. He was staring over the bridge into the water beneath. "Hey, take a look down there!"

Tiger and Kerry peered over the low bridge wall into

the murky waters of Blackshaw River. There, floating motionless on the surface, were half a dozen dead fish, their glazed eyes staring skywards. More dead fish floated a few metres away and Kerry drew back from the wall, holding her nose in disgust.

"This is serious," said Tiger, rubbing his chin thoughtfully. "We're only just at the start of the fishing season. Something must have got into the river. The water's been polluted. It could poison every living thing round here. We've got to tell someone and get something done about it!"

"Tiger," said Kerry, looking around suddenly. "Where's Scratch? He wouldn't go near the water, would he?"

The colour drained from Tiger's face. He stood motionless for a moment and then raised his hands to his mouth and yelled at the top of his voice. "Sc–rat–ch! Come here, Scratch! Sc–rat–ch!"

Tiger raced from the bridge and his voice once again shattered the evening stillness.

"Sc–rat–ch! Where are you, Scratch?"

"He's there," said Sam, pointing from the bridge. "I can see him, Tiger. He's by that fisherman along the bank. In fact, he seems to be making a bit of a nuisance of himself."

The fisherman had packed up and was doing his best to leave. However, Scratch seemed to think he was playing some sort of game and the more the fisherman tried to chase him away, the more excited Scratch was becoming.

"I'll go and get him," said Tiger. "He's only trying to be friendly." He started off towards the fisherman.

Then the strangest thing happened. As soon as the fisherman saw the boy approaching, he turned tail and ran. He ran as fast as he could in the opposite direction and, as he ran, he dropped something from his back pack – a fairly large object which fell into the grass without the fisherman noticing.

Tiger slowed down as Scratch bounded towards him and the fisherman disappeared into the distance towards Blackshaw Quarry. Tiger walked up to the spot where he had seen the object fall and moved the rough grass around with his training shoe. He could find nothing at first but he continued his search until his foot touched against something solid. It was a tin, an oblong tin, old and dented, with a tightly fitted lid. Tiger picked it up and examined it carefully. He shook it and something inside moved and rattled. He pulled at the lid but it was jammed on so tightly that he could not budge it.

"What's that?" said Sam, as he and Kerry approached.

"Did you see that?" said Tiger, completely ignoring Sam. "That fisherman ran off as soon as I got close – very strange if you ask me. He dropped this."

Tiger held the tin up for Sam and Kerry to see. "There's something inside but I can't get the lid off. It's well and truly stuck!"

"We'll have to take it home and force it open," said Sam.

"Good idea," said Tiger and he reached into his

pocket for Scratch's lead. "Come on, Scratch. We'll have you on a lead going home. I don't want you going near the water."

Tiger reached down a hand to grab the dog's collar and then he jumped back and let out a gasp.

"What's the matter?" said Kerry grabbing hold of Sam's arm.

"It's gone!" said Tiger, a distressed look on his face. "Scratch's new collar! He's gone and lost it!"

The dog wafted his long tail backwards and forwards and if the children hadn't known better, they would have sworn he was grinning at them.

—Chapter 3—

Another shock

Tiger, Sam and Kerry arrived early at school the following morning. They wanted to talk to somebody about what they had seen at Blackshaw River and Mrs Wilson seemed the obvious person to approach. Tiger had the 'Keep It Clean' kit tucked firmly underneath his arm. The children headed straight for Mrs Wilson's classroom. She was already sitting at her desk, marking books. Tiger knocked at the door and the children entered.

"Hello," said Mrs Wilson, looking up from her work. "Come in for an early start, have you? I heard about your bit of excitement, Tahir."

"Can we talk to you, Miss?" said Tiger, approaching the teacher's desk. "You said we could always come and see you if ever we had a problem."

"Of course you can talk to me," said Mrs Wilson, putting her pen down and folding her arms. "What is it you want to see me about?"

"Well, first of all, Miss, I've brought our 'Keep It Clean' kit from the building society."

Tiger handed over the cardboard box.

"Thank you, Tahir. Thank you very much. Good of you to remember with all that excitement."

"Get on with it," said Kerry, prodding Tiger in the ribs.

"Yes, well you see, Miss, Sam and Kerry and I went down to the river yesterday evening. We were standing on the bridge when Kerry saw all the rubbish lying around. There was all sorts, Miss – spare tyres, an old pram, all sorts of junk."

"It made me think about the 'Keep It Clean' campaign," said Kerry. "Something should be done to clean up the area around the river."

"Yes," said Mrs Wilson, slowly. "Well, maybe we can talk about this when we next discuss our topic, later today."

"No, Miss, you don't understand. It was then that we noticed the smell."

"The smell?" repeated Mrs Wilson, scratching her head.

"Yes, Miss," said Sam. "And when we looked into the river there were dead fish floating on the surface."

"What are you trying to tell me?" said Mrs Wilson.

"We think something's got into the river and polluted the water, Miss, and we want to know what to do about it."

"That's a sweeping statement to make with only a few dead fish for evidence," said Mrs Wilson. "It hardly amounts to proof of pollution, does it?"

"I know that river," said Tiger. "I go fishing there regularly. I can tell you that something's got into that water."

"Fishing rod … " said Sam thoughtfully. "Why was that man fishing for dead fish?"

Tiger stared at Sam and then waited for Mrs Wilson's reply.

"All right," said Mrs Wilson, "I'll make a few enquiries. That's all I can promise you. In the meantime … "

Mrs Wilson did not get the chance to finish her sentence for, suddenly, the classroom door burst open and Lucy Hollins tumbled inside, panting heavily, her face red with exertion. Behind her a group of children crowded the corridor and peered through the open doorway.

"Miss! Miss! You've got to come quickly!" gulped Lucy. "It's the conservation area! It's in an awful mess! Someone's wrecked it on purpose, Miss!"

Mrs Wilson leapt from her chair and rushed towards the classroom door, almost knocking Kerry over in her haste. She strode along the corridor with a string of children stretching out behind her. It was like a scene from the 'Pied Piper of Hamelin', with Tiger, Sam and Kerry at the back of the line doing their best to keep up with the pace.

Mrs Wilson marched through the main door and kept straight on across the playground, her crowd of followers growing by the minute. She swung open the gate to the conservation area and then stopped dead in her tracks, as if struck by lightning.

The scene that met her eyes did, indeed, resemble the wreckage of some great storm. Every newly planted sapling had been uprooted and snapped in half; Mrs Wilson's prize shrubs had been slashed and shredded, the remnants scattered across the area; one of the school bins had been emptied over the wall and there was litter everywhere; a can of gold spray paint had been used on the stone wall surrounding the area and the words 'WHAT A LOAD OF RUBBISH' were there for all to see. Worst of all, however, was the pond. The pond that had taken so much effort to dig out and line and stock was completely devastated. A metal spike wrenched from nearby railings had penetrated the lining so that all the water had drained away; bricks and rubble had been thrown into the empty shell and the whole area resembled a battleground.

"Senseless," murmured Mrs Wilson as she took a few paces into the conservation area. "Absolutely senseless."

A sea of silent faces peered through the gate and over the wall. Kerry pushed her way through the crowd and stood at the teacher's side.

"We can fix it, can't we?" she said, taking in the full extent of the devastation. "We will be able to fix it, won't we?"

Mrs Wilson smiled and looked down at her.

"Of course we'll fix it," she said. "We're not going to let them beat us, are we?"

The first lesson that Tuesday morning was a very subdued affair. The children at Pebble Street were shocked and angry. It was their hard work that had been destroyed and they were numbed by the whole experience.

At morning break, the playground was unusually quiet. Tiger, Sam and Kerry met on the far side of the yard by the wall.

"It's all falling apart," said Tiger. "We only got going on our topic yesterday and it's turning into a disaster. Things are worse now than before the building society started its 'Keep It Clean' campaign – and what's more, Scratch has lost his collar!"

"Don't be like that," said Kerry. "If everyone gave in so easily, this town would be in a right mess! You've got to show that you care."

"Mr Crompton cares," said Lucy Hollins, joining them." My mum says everyone should vote for Jonathan Crompton in the elections because he really cares about the environment."

Sam's ears pricked up and his face broke into a broad grin.

"Is that so?" he said, scratching his chin thoughtfully. "Jonathan Crompton really cares, does he?"

"He does, too," said Lucy. "He's holding a meeting in our school hall this week. You should come and listen to him."

"If Mr Crompton really does care," said Sam, "he won't mind if we visit him and tell him about the river, will he? He'll be only too pleased to listen to us."

"Brilliant!" said Tiger, cheering up immediately. "We'll do it tonight, after school. I've got to go back down to the river to look for Scratch's collar but we'll visit Mr Crompton first."

"Problem is," said Kerry, "we don't know where he lives, do we?"

"I know where he lives," said Lucy. "My mum went to pick up some leaflets from his house and I went with her. She's handing them out for the elections. In fact, I think I've got one on me."

Lucy fumbled in the pocket of her grey pinafore dress and produced a piece of paper folded in four. She opened it out and handed it to Tiger.

" 'Crompton Cares'," said Tiger, reading from the leaflet. "Nice photograph. He looks all right."

The face on the photograph was that of a middle-aged man. He had dark hair and a small moustache and he was smiling. Tiger thought that Mr Crompton looked like a man he could trust; a man who would listen.

"Yes, we'll definitely give Mr Crompton a try," said Tiger, handing back the leaflet. "Where does he live, Lucy?"

"He lives at 'The Grange'," said Lucy. "Big, detached house up on Thicketford Road. You can't miss it. He's got 'Crompton Cares' posters plastered all over the place."

"We'll find it," said Tiger, nodding his head up and down. "We'll find it."

The school bell rang for the end of morning play and just as the children were making their way to the school entrance, a leering face appeared above the school wall.

"Nothing wrong, is there?" said Vetch.

His voice was taunting and sarcastic. Kaz and Ginger appeared on either side of him silly grins on their faces.

"You know very well there's something wrong," said Sam with sudden realisation. "I don't suppose you did a bit of gardening last night, did you?"

"Gardening?" said Vetch, scratching his head. "No. If you ask me gardening's for old men. I've got much better things to do with my time."

"Yeah, gardening's for old men," repeated Ginger and then he thought for a moment before adding, "and old women, too, come to think of it."

"Vetch told you the trees wouldn't grow," said Kaz, a sneering grin on her face. "He was right, wasn't he?"

"Shut up, Kaz!" snapped Vetch.

"That's very interesting," said Sam, taking a step forward. "I bet Mrs Wilson would be very interested in what you said."

"You can't prove a thing," said Vetch, prodding a finger in Sam's direction. "Nobody can prove a thing." And he spat into the playground before disappearing from view behind the school wall.

"He's right, " said Kerry, as the children turned away. "We really can't prove a thing."

"I know we can't actually prove it – not yet," said Sam, "but *we* know who wrecked our conservation area and now we can have a go at proving it."

It was quite a walk to Thicketford Road. Tiger had bolted his tea down and called for Sam and Kerry soon after five o'clock. The sky was already dull and darker clouds seemed to be drifting towards the town from the direction of Blackshaw Moors.

"We'll come down to the river with you after we've seen Mr Crompton," said Sam. "I'd like to have another look round."

"Where's Scratch?" asked Kerry. "It's not like you to come out without him."

"I'm not having Scratch turn up at Mr Crompton's house with no collar on," replied Tiger. "It's his own fault. Until that collar's found, he stays at home."

Tiger stopped in his tracks as a persistent, high-pitched yapping invaded the early-evening peace.

"Don't I know that bark?" said Kerry, turning in the direction of the sound.

Sure enough, Scratch was cantering along the road towards the children, his head in the air and moving from side to side every time he barked.

"Scratch!" said Tiger, doing his best to sound annoyed. "I said you couldn't come. How did you get out?"

"I don't think he's going to answer you," said Sam, looking down at the dog.

"Well, we've no time to take him back now," said Kerry. "He'll have to come with us. Keep him away from Mr Crompton's house, though. He might not like to see us turn up with a dog not wearing a collar and lead."

"Yes, you're right," said Tiger thoughtfully. "Scratch can stay outside the gate."

There was no mistaking 'The Grange'. As the children

approached, there seemed to be posters everywhere. They were in the windows, on the walls, even attached to the trees in the garden.

Tiger made Scratch sit down outside the garden gate and said in his sternest voice, "You stay there, Scratch. Stay there!"

The dog looked disappointed but he sat and watched as the children walked confidently up the path and knocked on Mr Crompton's front door. There was a brief pause before the door opened and a cheerful-looking lady with light blonde curls appeared.

"Yes, what can I do for you?" she enquired.

"We'd like to see Mr Crompton, please," said Sam. "If it's not too much trouble, that is."

"Well, I'm Mrs Crompton," she said, opening the door a little wider. "May I ask what it is about?"

"It's about pollution," said Sam. "We know how much Mr Crompton cares about the environment and we think we've found something very serious. We really would like to talk to Mr Crompton if possible."

"Oh,' said Mrs Crompton, somewhat taken aback. "Jonathan's very busy but I'll see what I can do, then. You'd better come inside. There's a funny-looking stray dog mooching around by the gate and I don't like the look of it."

With that, the children stepped into the hallway and Mrs Crompton closed the door behind them.

—Chapter 4—
Figures in the dark

"You can rest assured that I will have this incident investigated," said Mr Crompton as he walked towards the gates of 'The Grange' with Sam, Tiger and Kerry. He pointed to the nearest poster attached to a tree.

"Crompton cares, you know. It's not just an empty slogan. I really do care about the environment and I will have this matter investigated to the full."

Mr Crompton stopped in his tracks and stared towards the gates. Scratch was lying across the pavement with his head on his paws. As he caught sight of Tiger, his tail began to beat slowly.

"Good heavens!" said Mr Crompton. "That creature doesn't belong to you, does it?"

"Never seen it before," lied Sam. "Your wife thinks it must be a stray."

"Perhaps she's right," said Mr Crompton, staring down at the dog. "It doesn't appear to be wearing a collar. Anyway, I must get back to the house now. Lots of work to do. Don't forget what I said – keep well away from that river. We don't want anyone poisoned, do we?"

"Thanks for your help," said Sam, as Mr Crompton backed away down the drive.

"Yes, and good luck in the elections!" shouted Kerry.

"Thanks a lot," said Mr Crompton and, with a wave of

his hand, he disappeared back into his house.

"I think he's nice," said Kerry, turning to face Tiger, "promising to investigate like that."

"I'm not so sure about him or his wife," said Tiger. Did you hear what they said about Scratch? A stray indeed! Anyone can see that Scratch isn't a stray."

At this point the dog stood up, yawned and scratched behind his left ear.

"Come on," said Sam, laughing. "Let's go home before it gets too dark."

"Home?" said Tiger, sounding surprised. "I'm not going home. I don't care what Mr Crompton said, I'm going down to the river to look for Scratch's collar and I'm going now before it gets any darker."

With that, he strode away from Sam and Kerry, Scratch trailing after him, his tail wafting from side to side in the evening air.

The light was fading fast by the time the children reached the river. The darker clouds that had been gathering earlier that evening loomed overhead and the first few drops of rain were beginning to fall from the leaden sky.

"I don't like rain," said Tiger, as the children stood on the stone bridge overlooking the water. "And Scratch hates it. He can't stand getting his coat wet."

"That's funny," said Kerry, staring over the bridge into the water. "The fish have gone."

"It's not that funny," said Sam. "A stray cat has

probably had them or maybe they've just sunk below the surface."

"Dead fish don't sink," said Tiger, "and if a cat has eaten them it will probably be a dead cat by now. Those fish were poisoned, don't forget."

"Look at that brown scum round the edge of the water," said Kerry. "It looks disgusting."

"Something's got into that river," said Tiger. "I know that water's polluted."

"Oh, let's get on with it," said Sam, irritably. "There's no way we'll find Scratch's collar if we don't start looking soon. It's getting dark."

"Come on, then," said Tiger. "Let's look down by where that strange man was fishing."

He walked off the bridge and strode out over the rough ground, Scratch trotting at his heels.

"That reminds me," said Kerry, chasing after Tiger. "What about the tin you found? Did you look inside it?"

"Couldn't get it open," said Tiger, scanning the ground for Scratch's collar. "The lid's jammed on tight."

"Bring it round later," said Sam. "We'll have a go at it together."

The children reached the spot where the fisherman had been sitting the previous evening but, despite a thorough search, there was no sign of the collar.

After about fifteen minutes, Sam said, "Come on, you two. It really is starting to get dark. We'll never find anything in this light."

"I suppose you're right," said Tiger, reluctantly. "Let's

head for home. We can go up through the quarry and on to the top road. It'll be too dark to go back the other way."

The children took a rough track that followed the water's edge. The brown foam that they had seen from the bridge seemed to skirt the length of the river and Tiger was careful to keep Scratch well away from the water. The weather had deteriorated and the drops of rain that had fallen earlier had developed into a steady drizzle.

"It's not far now," said Tiger, pulling up the collar on his thin, nylon jacket. "We just follow this stream up into the quarry. We can see the road from there."

Then he stopped suddenly, causing Sam and Kerry to pull up abruptly.

"What's the matter?" said Kerry. "Why have you stopped?"

"The stream," said Tiger, slowly. He reached down to make sure Scratch was at his heels. "Look at the stream."

Sam and Kerry followed Tiger's gaze to where a small stream, usually no more than a steady trickle of water, wound its way under a small, wooden footbridge to join the river.

"Ugh! It's horrible!" said Kerry. "It looks like dirty, greasy, washing-up water. And it's got that foam on it. It's horrible!"

"Yes, and it's feeding into the river," said Tiger. "It runs down from the quarry into the river."

"Listen!" said Sam, grabbing hold of Tiger's arm. "I'm sure I can hear something! Listen!"

The children stood in silence and listened into the gloom. There were voices, several voices, and somewhere there was an engine running. The voices were not shouting or chatting, they were short and sharp as if giving and receiving instructions.

"I don't like it," said Kerry as the drizzle fell steadily. "It's really eerie."

"It's all right," said Tiger. "Let's go quietly and follow the stream into the quarry. It's probably just a group of people up on the road."

The children moved forward. Tiger went first with Scratch still at his heels. The track followed the stream up into the quarry but, as they drew nearer, Tiger stopped again. There could be no doubt that the voices were coming from the quarry, not from the road above. Tiger signalled to Sam and Kerry to keep quiet and then beckoned them forward to a cluster of hawthorn bushes. The children stooped down and peered around the bushes, directly into the quarry.

The sight that met their eyes could have been taken straight from a science fiction film. The quarry was alive with figures, six or seven strange, hooded figures that moved methodically and pointed some sort of an instrument down at the ground in front of them. Up on the road, overlooking the very edge of the quarry, was a vehicle. Its headlights cast an eerie, yellow glow into the pit and gave some of the figures, huge, distorted shadows that leapt and grew and then disappeared as they changed position. Scratch began to growl, low and rumbling, and Tiger put his arm round the dog's neck to quieten him.

"Who are they?" whispered Sam, edging nearer to Tiger. "What are they doing?"

"I don't know," replied Tiger, his voice low and trembling. "I can't see properly from here. I need to be closer."

"No, don't," said Kerry. "You'll be caught!"

"Put your arm round Scratch," said Tiger, ignoring Kerry. "Hold him tight so that he doesn't follow me. See that bush over there? I'm going to try and get to it so I can see better."

"Tiger, don't ... " began Kerry but it was too late, for Tiger had darted forward and, keeping low to the ground, he raced across a small clearing before diving for cover behind the bush.

Tiger could see much more clearly from his new position. Two of the figures were no more than ten metres away from him and he was able to study them in detail. They were dressed in some sort of protective clothing – lightweight suits that covered the whole of their bodies, gloves that overlapped their sleeves and hoods with a Perspex front for vision. They each carried some sort of small pack on their backs and this was connected by a short length of tubing to a long stick which they held in their hands. Tiger watched carefully and, every so often, he would see a spray of liquid spurt

from the end of the sticks. Then Tiger glanced upwards and he could see that something was being hoisted up the wall of the quarry. At first, it was just a dark shape, difficult to distinguish against the dark grey background of the quarry wall but, after a few moments of concentration, Tiger could make out that it was a container of some sort, a little bit like a metal dustbin.

"It can't be a dustbin," thought Tiger. "Why would hooded men want to haul a dustbin up a quarry wall? It doesn't make sense!"

Back at the edge of the quarry, Scratch was getting restless. He didn't see why he couldn't be with Tiger and he began to wriggle and whine in an attempt to loosen Sam's grip. Tiger heard him – but it was too late. One of the hooded men stopped and turned and then pointed towards the hawthorn bushes at the edge of the quarry. Tiger felt a cold chill run down his spine as the hooded figure took a step forward and peered into the gloom. As he strained to see into the darkness, something darted out towards him from the cover of the bushes. Scratch had broken free and, despite Sam's desperate efforts to grab him and pull him back, the dog had escaped his clutches and darted into the quarry.

The hooded figures stepped back at first, then, startled into action, they rushed towards the dog. One of them picked up a piece of rock and hurled it towards Scratch, missing his head by a fraction. Before he realised what he had done, Tiger leapt out from behind the bush and yelled at the figure.

"Don't you dare throw rocks at my dog!"

The figure whipped off his protective hood and stared at the boy, their eyes meeting in the moment's silence, before he bellowed out across the quarry.

"There's a kid here! He's been watching us!"

A voice from the top of the quarry shouted, "Get him!" and the words echoed and thundered and grew in the hollow darkness.

The figure nearest to Tiger reacted first. He leapt forward and grabbed the boy before Tiger knew what had happened. Scratch immediately bit the man's leg, causing him to loosen his grip and shriek in pain. At the same time there was a tremendous crash at the far end of the quarry. The rope holding the metal drum had slipped and the container had crashed to the ground.

There was a panic of voices as the hooded figures turned towards the fallen container.

Tiger took his chance. He lashed out with his arm, causing his captor to stagger backwards. Tiger turned and ran. He ran as fast as he could, racing out of the quarry, past Sam and Kerry who leapt to their feet and followed him immediately.

The children ran and ran, charging breathlessly through the darkness, stumbling over the rough ground, and they didn't dare stop until the chaos of the quarry was far behind them in the closing darkness of night.

—Chapter 5—
Tiger's tin

Only when they reached the safety of the stone bridge did the children stop their charge away from the quarry. Tiger sank to the ground, gasping for breath, taking in the cold evening air in great gulps. Sam and Kerry sprawled across the stone wall, unable to speak for a few moments until they had recovered their composure. And there, at the far end of the bridge, wagging his long, hairy tail as if nothing out of the ordinary had happened, was Scratch.

Tiger dragged himself to his feet when he caught sight of the dog.

"You really did it that time, didn't you, Scratch? Why didn't you stay out of the way with Sam?"

"Let's get home," said Kerry. She sounded exhausted. "We'll talk about things when we get home."

It was twenty minutes later when Sam glanced at his watch and said,

"We're late. It's gone half past seven. Mum said we had to be in by seven o'clock."

"She won't mind too much," said Kerry. "Gary's coming round to do her hair tonight."

"Can I come round?" asked Tiger. "We need to talk and I'd rather come round to your house."

"You'll have to take Scratch home first," said Kerry. "You know he doesn't get on with our cat."

Five minutes later Tiger had deposited Scratch and emerged from his house carrying the tin dropped by the lone fisherman the previous evening.

"I thought we could try to open it," he explained.

A hideous, bright orange car was parked outside Sam and Kerry's house and, as they approached, Tiger looked at it in distaste.

"It's awful, isn't it?" said Sam. "It belongs to Gary. You'll understand when you see him."

"I can't wait," said Tiger and they went into the house and closed the front door behind them.

"There's a funny smell in here," said Tiger, sniffing the air. "I'm sure I can smell something funny."

"It's Gary, the hairdresser," explained Kerry. "I don't mean it's *him* – it's the stuff he uses on my mum's hair. Come into the kitchen and have a look."

Tiger twitched his nose in disgust and followed Kerry along the small hallway and into the kitchen. Mrs Simpson was sitting on a wooden chair that had been positioned near the kitchen sink. Tiger stopped in amazement when he saw her and then his face broke into a slow, spreading smile. Mrs Simpson had what looked like a polythene cap on her head. There were holes in the cap and bits of her hair had been pulled through and plastered with a foul-smelling, blue paste. She had a gaudy beach towel wrapped around her shoulders and bits of hair littered the floor at her feet.

Gary, the hairdresser, was leaning against the sink drinking coffee. He had a pleasant, round face and dark, spiky hair that looked as though it needed a good cut. As the children entered, he smiled at them and took a sip of his drink. He looked most contented.

"Hello," said Mrs Simpson. "You're a bit late in, you know. I did say seven o'clock."

"Sorry, Mum," said Sam. "We, er … we lost track of the time."

"Well, no harm done, I suppose." Then, looking at Tiger, she said, "I'm getting my hair done, Tahir. You'll have to excuse the mess."

"It's OK," said Tiger. "I'm sure it will look very nice."

"Another twenty minutes and she'll look like a new woman," said Gary.

"That'll take a miracle, not a haircut," grunted Mr Simpson. He was sitting at the kitchen table and the voice came from somewhere behind his newspaper.

Mrs Simpson said something the children didn't quite catch.

Tiger was looking thoughtful.

"You know, Scratch could do with a haircut now that spring has arrived. I don't suppose you do dogs, Gary?"

"I could give him a perm for you," said Gary seriously. "Very reasonable rates and I'd make a lovely job of it."

"No, I don't think he'd suit a perm," said Tiger. "Perhaps I'd better leave it for now."

"Come on," said Sam, tugging at Tiger's arm. "Let's go upstairs and sort out the other business, shall we?"

"Good idea," said Tiger and he backed out of the

kitchen, still twitching his nose in distaste at the peculiar smell coming from Mrs Simpson's hair.

Once they were up in Sam's bedroom, the conversation turned to the strange events witnessed earlier that evening.

"We've got to do something," said Kerry. "We can't just ignore what we saw."

"Yes, but what *did* we see?" said Sam. "We saw some men working in a quarry. We don't know that they were doing anything wrong."

"It doesn't take a genius to guess what they were up to," said Kerry. "The river gets polluted, a stream leads from the quarry to the river, we see men taking containers from the quarry and walking around in protective clothing spraying the ground. It doesn't take a genius, does it?"

"Yes, but what do we do about it?" said Sam.

"We go straight back to the quarry tomorrow morning," said Kerry, "before all the evidence disappears. We can take your camera, Sam, and get some pictures."

"What about school?" said Sam.

"This is much more important," said Tiger. If we're quick we'll only be about half an hour late. We can go straight to Mrs Wilson and tell her the whole story. She'll know what to do next."

"All right," said Sam. "We'll go back tomorrow morning. Now, let's see if we can get this tin open."

"I've been trying," said Tiger, pulling at the lid, "but it's really stuck. It's not empty, though. You can hear something inside if you shake it."

"Let me have a go," said Sam and he took the tin from Tiger and tried to force the lid off.

It was no use. The lid was jammed on tight and, no matter how hard Sam strained, he could not get it to budge.

Eventually he said, "Let's go down to the kitchen and run it under the hot water tap. That should do the trick."

"Good idea," said Tiger, and he took the tin back from Sam and set off down the stairs.

As the children entered the kitchen, Gary was putting the finishing touches to Mrs Simpson's hair.

"That looks good, Mum," said Kerry, nodding her approval.

"Yes, very nice, Mrs Simpson," agreed Tiger, waving the tin in the air. Mrs Simpson beamed with pleasure.

"What have you got there?" said Gary, pointing to Tiger's tin.

'Oh, it's ... er ... just a tin," said Tiger. "It was dropped by a fisherman down by the river. We can't get the lid off."

"I do a bit of fishing myself," said Gary, looking interested. "Give it here and I'll see if I can get it open for you."

Tiger passed the tin over Mrs Simpson's shoulder and Gary looked at it curiously.

"I've got a tin something like this," he said as he began to pull at the lid. "I always take it when I go fishing. No fisherman would be without one." His face was turning purple with the effort. "I think it's coming … it's coming … "

It was then that the chaos began, for the lid flew off with an almighty 'pop' and little yellow-white blobs cascaded out of the tin. They flew into the air and rained down all over the kitchen. When Mrs Simpson realised what they were, she let out a scream that could be heard the length of the street.

"Maggots!" she cried and she leapt to her feet as the soft, wriggling bodies landed all over her. "They're in my hair! I can feel them! Get them off me! Get them off!"

"Don't panic!" shouted Gary. "Don't panic! They can't do any harm!"

"Ugh! They're horrible!" shouted Kerry, brushing a cluster of yellow bodies off her clothes.

Mr Simpson leapt from his seat at the kitchen table, rolled up his paper and began hitting Mrs Simpson on the head with it.

"Don't panic!" shouted Gary, waving his arms around. "They really won't harm you!"

The yellow-white maggots were everywhere. They were writhing on the floor; they were squirming in the sink. They had landed on the table and were floating in the dregs of Gary's coffee.

Mrs Simpson was beside herself and, when she finally regained a semblance of self-control, she pointed an accusing finger at Tiger and said, "It's that blessed boy! He's brought maggots into my house!"

"Yes, well, er … I'd better be going now," said Tiger, backing towards the door. "I'll, er … I'll see you tomorrow."

With that, Tiger fled from the kitchen, banging the door behind him.

It was a clear, spring morning. The grey drizzle of the previous evening had been replaced by a fresh, blue sky. The sun was shining and the air already felt warm.

"Mum was furious," said Kerry, chewing a piece of toast that was left over from breakfast. "She made Dad and Sam clear all the maggots up and then she made Gary wash her hair again. She was really furious."

"I don't see why she blamed me," said Tiger, as they walked along. "I didn't open the stupid tin, did I?"

"Let's get a move on," said Kerry, "before anyone sees us. Got the camera, Sam?"

"Yes," said Sam, patting his shoulder bag. "There's about five snaps left on the film."

It was not long before they reached the stone bridge overlooking Blackshaw River. It was a very different scene from that of the previous evening. The early morning sunshine glistened and sparkled on the water and the whole picture was one of peace and tranquillity. Only the brown rim along the edge of the water gave any clue that something was wrong.

"Take a picture of it," said Tiger. "Down there beneath the bridge where that foam has gathered."

Sam took the photograph and the children dropped from the bridge on to the path leading towards the quarry. About half-way along, Tiger pulled up suddenly and pointed at a cluster of thistles.

"I don't believe it," he said. "Look at that!"

There, nestling close to the ground, was Scratch's collar, damp and slightly faded but perfectly intact.

"He'll be so pleased," said Tiger, shaking the collar and putting it in his jacket pocket. "Scratch really liked that collar."

A few more minutes took the children to the hawthorn bushes at the edge of the quarry. They crept forward, half-expecting to see the strange hooded figures that had peopled the quarry the previous evening.

However, all was quiet. The quarry was deserted. The children advanced slowly, aware that even in the bright morning sunshine the quarry had an eerie atmosphere that sent shivers down their spines.

They stood in the very centre of the quarry and listened to the silence. Then that silence was suddenly shattered as a piercing yell tore into the quarry and echoed round and round the enclosed space, causing Sam, Tiger and Kerry to cling to each other in fright. The yell subsided and the three children stood rooted to the spot wondering what on earth was going to happen next.

—Chapter 6—

Trouble with Vetch

The first yell was followed by a second yell and then a third yell was followed by a series of whoops and screams and crashing rocks. The three children recovered quickly from their first fright and, as Sam moved away from Tiger and his sister, he said, "It's coming from over there, around the other side of the quarry."

"Let's go and look," said Tiger.

The children edged forward until they could peer around the quarry wall. On the other side of the wall the land was like a refuse tip. Rubbish was piled high, tipped from the road above and there, on top of the rubbish, whooping at the top of his voice, was Vetch. Kaz was a few metres below him, pushing Ginger round and round the heap in a broken pram. Every so often, Kaz screamed as Vetch hurled a piece of rubbish in her direction.

"It's horrible," said Kerry. "They're as bad as each other."

"Look at the wall behind them," said Tiger, slowly. "Where have you seen a message sprayed in gold paint recently?"

"The conservation area," said Sam. "You're right. If I can just get a picture – he's even signed his name in gold."

"Let's give it a try," said Tiger. "We've got nothing to lose."

Tiger stepped out into full view, Sam and Kerry following close behind. Vetch spotted them immediately.

"Well, look who it is," he said from his vantage point on top of the rubbish heap. "It's my little gardening friends."

He leapt down from the heap in three great strides and stood directly in front of Tiger.

"Come and have a look, Kaz! Come and have a look, Ginger!"

"What are you doing here?" snapped Kaz, prodding a finger towards Sam. "Why aren't you at school?"

"We're here as part of our project," said Sam quickly and he produced the camera from his bag. "We've come to take photos of the quarry and the river. It's an area we think we can tidy up, you see."

"Daft idea," said Ginger, sniffing and wiping his nose on his sleeve. "What do you want to tidy it up for?"

"We like it as it is," said Vetch, turning and smiling at his friends. "It's more fun, see?"

"Yeah, it's more fun," repeated Ginger. "If you tidied it up there wouldn't be any rubbish, would there?"

Tiger glanced at Sam but decided not to reply.

"Anyway, seeing as you're here," said Vetch, "perhaps you'd like to take a picture of me? Yeah, you can take a picture of me and Kaz – and Ginger for that matter. Ginger likes having his photo taken, don't you, Ginger?"

"Not really," said Ginger, looking puzzled.

"Well, it would fit in with our project on pollution," said Sam, seriously. "The light's wrong here, though. If you stand by that wall it should be just right."

Vetch, Kaz and Ginger obligingly moved towards the graffiti and Sam lined them up carefully and took his picture.

"Thanks very much," said Sam, replacing the camera in his bag. "It'll come in very useful."

The children backed away, leaving Vetch and his friends to play among the rubbish.

"We may not have found exactly what we came for," said Tiger when they were back in the main quarry, "but I'm sure Mrs Wilson will want to see that particular photograph."

"There's nothing else here," said Sam. "Let's get to school."

"There's a path that goes round the side of the quarry up to the top road," said Tiger. "It'll be quicker than going back the other way."

The children had one last look around the quarry and then made their way towards the rough track that Tiger had indicated. It was fairly steep and, as it was still damp from the previous night's drizzle, it was, in parts, quite slippery. However, it was not long before the road was in sight and, as the children neared the top, they could still hear the strange, animal sounds from Vetch and his friends far below them.

Tiger was leading the way and he was just about to step out on to the road when he stopped suddenly and raised a warning hand.

Sam and Kerry came up close behind him and Kerry said, "What's the matter, Tiger? Why have you stopped?"

"There's a truck," said Tiger, his voice low and suspicious. "It's pulled up on the road above the quarry just where that truck stopped last night. I'm sure it's the same one."

"Let me see," said Sam, pushing past and keeping low to the ground.

Sure enough, a large truck had pulled off the road and stopped at the very edge of the quarry. The words 'TETROCHEM LTD' were painted on the driver's door and underneath was the address, 'Red Lane, Blackshaw'. Two men were standing a few metres from the truck, staring down into the empty quarry.

Tiger nudged Sam and whispered, "Take a picture."

"I've only got three left,' said Sam, producing his camera again.

"Take a picture," repeated Tiger. "It's just what we want. It's evidence, Sam."

Sam lined the camera up, making sure that he got both men and the truck in the frame before his finger squeezed the button and the shutter clicked quietly.

"That only leaves two," said Sam. "I've only two left now."

The children watched and waited for another five minutes as the men surveyed the quarry beneath them. Then, as quickly as they had arrived, they climbed back into their truck and drove away.

"What do you make of that?" said Kerry as they clambered up on to the road.

"Very suspicious," said Tiger. "They were probably checking that everything was all right."

"I think we need to talk to Mrs Wilson again," said Sam. "I'm sure she'll listen when we tell her what we've seen."

"Let's get cleaned up first," said Kerry, looking at her hands and knees. "I'm filthy after climbing that path."

"Come on then," said Tiger, heading off along the road. "You can come back to my place – my mum's out at work. I can't wait to give Scratch his collar back. I just know he's going to be really pleased."

"I bet he will," said Sam, and he and Kerry followed their friend along the road towards Blackshaw.

The bell for the start of the afternoon session was just ringing when Sam, Tiger and Kerry arrived in the school playground. They had washed and had a sandwich at Tiger's house and by the time Tiger had struggled to put Scratch's collar back on, the morning had gone.

"We'll see Mrs Wilson as soon as we go in," said Sam. "We'll see if we can get this business sorted."

It was not to be. As Sam and Tiger entered their classroom they saw, not the familiar figure of Mrs Wilson at the front of the class, but the less-welcome form of the Reverend Humphrey Snelling, vicar of Blackshaw Parish Church.

"What's he doing here?" said Tiger, as Richard Hooper pushed past him. "Where's Mrs Wilson?"

"She's on a course for two days," said Richard. "Some sort of training, the vicar said."

"Now then!" shouted the Reverend Snelling, clapping his hands. "Let us settle down, shall we? It's a beautiful spring afternoon and we have work to do."

The vicar clasped his hands together and beamed at the class.

"I know that we were all disappointed to find that the conservation area had been vandalized but we must not be disheartened, must we? We must look upon such an act as a temporary setback. If we are going to encourage all of God's little creatures into our conservation area, we must be determined to succeed. For that reason, we shall go out this afternoon and start to repair the damage. Now, what do you think of that?"

There was certainly a lot of work to be done and, as the vicar was not the best person at organisation, the children sorted themselves out. One group set about clearing the litter and debris. The vicar supplied them with transparent polythene gloves and black plastic bags and they started at one side of the conservation area and worked their way methodically across the ground.

A group of parents were helping some of the children to inspect the damaged saplings. Many of them were so badly broken that they were beyond repair but those that could be saved were bandaged carefully and attached to new, stronger stakes for extra support.

Another parent was working with a group of children at the pond. The metal spike had been removed and, once the dirt and rubble had been cleared away, it was decided that the pond could be patched.

There was also the compost heap. That had been Mrs Wilson's idea. She had started it the previous autumn by sectioning off an area next to the stone wall. The compost was to be spread on to a patch of ground reserved for growing vegetables and Tiger had volunteered Sam and himself to do the job.

"Thanks a lot," said Sam, as he stood back and watched Tiger peel away the black plastic cover from the top of the heap. "Of all the jobs we could do, you have to go and get us this one."

The compost heap began to steam as soon as it was exposed to the open air. Sam pulled a face and held his nose. "It's revolting, Tiger. It smells awful."

"Of course it doesn't," said Tiger, plunging his spade into the great steaming heap. "This is a lovely compost heap. If you look closely you can see that it's alive with worms. Little red ones, wriggling like mad."

"I don't want to get that close, thanks," said Sam. "I'll push the wheelbarrow if you don't mind."

Tiger shovelled the first spadeful of compost into the wheelbarrow and said, "Do you know, Catherine Hill's horse has helped to make this compost heap so rich. Every so often Catherine's brought along a plastic bucket full of … "

"I don't want to know," said Sam quickly.

"Please yourself!" said Tiger and he dropped another spadeful of compost into the barrow.

The wheelbarrow was almost full when Tiger and Sam were disturbed. Three familiar, leering faces appeared above the wall and, as Kaz spat her chewing gum out on to the compost heap, Vetch said in a mocking voice, "Working hard, are you? It's a pity about the mess. Lot of extra work, isn't it?"

"Well, you'd know all about the mess, wouldn't you?" said Sam.

"I don't know what you mean," said Vetch. "It's nothing to do with us. Anyway, there's a funny smell around here." He sniffed the air in an exaggerated manner. "That peculiar dog isn't around, is it?"

"Don't you insult Scratch," warned Tiger. "He's got more brains than you have."

"I've never seen such a funny-looking creature," said Vetch.

He could see that Tiger was getting worked up and he was beginning to enjoy himself. "Must be one of the ugliest animals I've ever seen."

It was too much for Tiger. His face had turned red with rage. He took a step forward and plunged his spade into the steaming, wet, compost heap. With one swift movement, the contents of the spade were flung upwards towards the wall and splattered into Vetch's face. There was a moment's stunned silence before Vetch let out a cry of despair that caused everyone to stop work and stare in his direction.

The wet, brown compost dripped from his face. A lump had lodged in his long, untidy hair and, in among the matted mess, red-pink worms could be seen wriggling and writhing. Kaz and Ginger just stared open-mouthed, a look of horror and disbelief on their faces. Vetch wiped a grubby hand across his mouth and then seemed to explode into a fit of temper.

"You just wait!" he stormed, pointing at Tiger. "I'll fix you and I'll fix that … that … creature of yours! You just see if I don't!"

A roar of laughter went up as the twenty-nine children from Mrs Wilson's class bellowed their approval at Tiger's action.

Vetch shook his fist in a final act of defiance and then dropped behind the wall and out of sight as Tiger once again plunged his spade into the compost heap, as if to reload his weapon.

—Chapter 7—

Journey into danger

"We got away with it once, we can do it again," said Tiger, as he stood outside the shop on the corner of the street.

It was the morning after Tiger had covered Vetch with compost.

"We've got to tell somebody about the river and the quarry and the men we saw," said Tiger. "Mrs Wilson's still not back at school today, the police won't want to know without proper evidence, so it makes sense to go back to Mr Crompton. He really cares. You both said he did – remember?"

"Yes, I know he cares," said Kerry, "but missing school again? I'm not sure."

"Nobody even noticed we were missing," said Tiger. "Old Snelling hasn't got a clue who's in and who's not."

"Well, my teacher noticed I was missing," said Kerry. "She told me I had to bring a note in this morning."

"Well, there you are then!" said Tiger.

"What do you mean 'there I am'?" snapped Kerry.

"If you don't go to school you can't give her a note, can you?" said Tiger. "Problem solved."

"I'm not sure," said Kerry. "I don't really like it."

"Look," said Tiger. "Do you think Mrs Wilson would like us to clean up the environment?"

"Well, yes, I suppose so," said Kerry.

"And would she want us to turn a blind eye if someone was ruining the environment?"

"Well, no I don't suppose she would," said Kerry.

"Well, there you are then!" said Tiger in triumph. "Problem solved!" He walked off down the road, leaving Sam and Kerry to follow in his footsteps.

The children took a roundabout route to Mr Crompton's house. It took them through back streets of terraced houses, away from the centre of Blackshaw. Eventually, they came out at the bottom end of Thicketford Road, about half a mile from 'The Grange'.

"We're all right here," said Sam, looking up and down the road. He was clutching his camera in his hand. He still had a couple of snaps left and he wanted to use them up so that the film could be developed.

"Nobody from school is going to recognise us around here."

"You're right," said Tiger and then he stopped suddenly and stared across the road in the direction of a small shop.

It was a newsagents and Sam and Kerry realised immediately what it was that Tiger had seen. A truck was parked outside the shop – a brown truck that had, printed on the driver's door, the words 'TETROCHEM LTD'.

"It's the same one," said Tiger, pointing across the road. "It's the same truck that was by the quarry! This is too good to miss!"

Before Sam and Kerry knew what was happening, Tiger dashed across the road, jumped on to the back of the truck and slid under the tarpaulin. A man came out of the shop almost immediately. He paused briefly, looked up and down the road and then climbed into the truck. The truck's engine coughed and then burst into life and, as Sam and Kerry stared helplessly, it drove off down the road, carrying its secret passenger out of sight.

"I don't believe it!" said Sam in amazement. "What did he want to go and do a stupid thing like that for?"

"He probably thinks the truck will take him to the factory," said Kerry. "At least he'll know where it is."

"We already had the name of the firm," said Sam in frustration. "It was on the side of the truck. That was all we needed. I'm sure Mr Crompton or the police would be able to trace it."

"He'll be all right," said Kerry, confidently. "He'll probably join up with us later. He just didn't think."

"He never thinks," snapped Sam. "That's the trouble with Tiger – he never thinks!"

A couple of minutes later, Sam and Kerry were standing on the path at the front of 'The Grange'. Mr Crompton's smiling face was staring at them from a poster in the front window and the now familiar 'Crompton Cares' slogan gave Kerry a feeling of warmth and security.

Beneath the large election poster was a smaller leaflet that also bore a picture of Mr Crompton and, as Kerry read the advertisement on the leaflet, she tugged at her brother's sleeve and said, "How about that, Sam? Mr Crompton's meeting is tonight. The one at our school, I mean. The one he was telling us about."

"Very nice," said Sam, totally disinterested, and he stepped forward and knocked confidently on Mr Crompton's front door.

There was a moment's pause before a bolt slid back and the door opened. Mr Crompton stood in the doorway, a rolled-up newspaper under his arm and a half-eaten piece of toast in his hand.

He stared at the children for a few seconds, his moustache twitched and then, in sudden recognition, he said,

"Ah! My friends from Pebble Street! Well, two of them at least. Don't just stand there, come inside!"

Sam and Kerry stepped into the hallway. Mr Crompton closed the door behind them and then ushered them into a room that appeared to be a study.

"You'll have to excuse the mess," said Mr Crompton, "but you'll understand that I'm very busy at the moment. In fact, I'm speaking at your school this evening. It was Pebble Street, wasn't it?"

"That's right," said Sam. "We noticed the leaflet in your window."

"Ah, yes," said Mr Crompton, pulling at his moustache, "I'm hoping for a good turn out tonight. Now then, what was it you wanted to see me about?"

"It's a follow-up to our last visit, really," said Kerry. "We know that a local firm has polluted Blackshaw River. We've got evidence this time. Sam's taken pictures and we saw men in the quarry, strange men wearing strange suits. They were spraying the ground and ... "

"Now just hold on a minute," said Mr Crompton.

He walked across the room and perched on the edge of his desk. "This sounds serious. More serious than I first thought. You say you have pictures?"

"That's right," said Sam and he held up his camera to

show Mr Crompton. "And we know the name of the firm responsible. I took a picture of their truck when it was parked above the quarry."

"You've done very well," said Mr Crompton. "I've started investigations as I promised I would, but I must say you've done very well indeed. We need to get this film developed as soon as possible. I'll take care of that for you."

Mr Crompton reached over and took hold of Sam's camera. He slid back the catch to release the back and shook out the cartridge. Having placed the film carefully in the top drawer of his desk, Mr Crompton said "That film could be vital if the police are going to prosecute this firm. Now, what other evidence have you got?"

"Well, nothing really," said Kerry. "But our friend could be learning something right now. You see, we spotted the same truck that was at the quarry outside your local newsagents and Tiger jumped on the back. The driver doesn't know he's there and ... "

"He did what?" interrupted Mr Crompton. His eyes widened and he looked worried. "What did you say he did?"

"He jumped on the back of the truck," repeated Kerry. "He'll be all right."

"All right?" said Mr Crompton, his voice rising, his moustache twitching. "All right? He could be in grave danger! You don't know what these people are like! If your friend is discovered, you don't know what might happen."

Sam and Kerry looked at each other nervously.

"We must act right away," continued Mr Crompton, jumping to his feet. "We must go to the police and get this firm traced. You come with me. I'll get this business sorted out once and for all!"

Mr Crompton rushed out of the room, leaving Sam and Kerry stunned and somewhat bewildered.

Tiger didn't really know why he had jumped on to the back of the truck but as he sat back underneath the tarpaulin cover, he was beginning to wonder whether or not he had made a mistake. The truck bumped and jolted its way through Blackshaw before turning right towards the industrial estate on the edge of town. Tiger knew he was heading for the industrial estate because he stuck his head up through a gap in the cover and peered over the side of the truck. He ducked down below the cover again as he felt the truck slow down. It went over some rough, bumpy ground, turned left into what Tiger guessed was a factory yard and then stopped suddenly, causing Tiger to lurch forward.

Tiger did not know what to do but, as there was nothing else beneath the cover, he decided he would stay hidden and keep his fingers crossed that he would not be discovered. He heard a voice, a high-pitched voice that sounded familiar.

"D'you want the door up, Jacko? Are you putting her inside?"

"Yeah, lift it up, will you!"

There was a scraping, scratching sound as if a rusty garage door was being raised and then a thump as it thudded into position. The truck pulled forward and then the engine juddered, cut and died. Tiger's heart began to beat faster. He heard the driver's door open and then felt the truck lurch as Jacko jumped from the cab. The door slammed shut and the noise seemed to echo and vibrate. Tiger could hear the sound of Jacko's footsteps. He was walking away from the truck. After a moment, the metal door clattered shut and Tiger was left alone in the silence.

Slowly, cautiously, Tiger poked his head through the gap in the tarpaulin cover and stared over the side of the truck. Everywhere was very quiet, strangely still for what Tiger felt sure was a factory. Tiger could see that he was in some sort of large storage building. Several vehicles were parked. There were two trucks, a transit van and a couple of cars towards the back of the building, partly obscured by a pile of cardboard boxes stacked on top of each other. Tiger ducked down below the cover and crawled out again towards the end of the truck. He sat for a moment, his legs dangling over the edge of the truck, and then he jumped down quietly on to the stone floor.

He looked around again. There were boxes everywhere – strong cardboard boxes, bound tightly with plastic strips, piled haphazardly on wooden platforms around the building. To the left of the drop-down door was a fork-lift truck, its lifting mechanism lying flat on the floor underneath one of the wooden platforms.

Tiger approached the drop-down door. He put his ear against it and listened for any sound from the other side. There was an engine running but Tiger could not hear any voices. It was strange. Why could he not hear the hustle and bustle he expected to hear from a working factory? Tiger looked up and down the door for the mechanism that would make it lift. He spotted a catch near the very top of the door. He doubted whether it would work but he had to try. He stood on tiptoe and strained upwards, only to find that his outstretched fingers were some way short of the catch. He relaxed and looked around quickly. A box! One of the boxes would do fine to stand on. Tiger took one from the nearest pile. It was heavier than he expected and he struggled to lift it down. Once on the concrete floor, he could push and manoeuvre the box until it was in just the right position.

Tiger climbed on top of the box and reached again for the catch but before he could touch it the door suddenly swung upwards and crashed against his shins. Tiger reeled backwards off the box, shouting out in pain. He crashed to the floor and felt his shoulder scrape and jolt on the rough concrete. Light flooded in from the open door and, as Tiger glanced up, he was confronted by three figures. One was Jacko, the driver of the truck. He was clutching a large stick and he took a step forward, raising the stick above his head. Tiger instinctively raised his hands and ducked his head but, in the split second he had before his vision was obscured,

Tiger caught sight of the other two figures. One was a man, of medium height and ordinary looking, probably the same man who had visited the quarry with Jacko, but the other figure was a woman, dressed, like Jacko, in blue overalls but definitely a woman. Tiger recognised her. He had seen her before. A picture flashed into his mind. A car parked on double yellow lines outside the Blackshaw Building Society – a distinctive maroon hatchback. The driver, wearing dark glasses and a khaki hat, the voice high pitched – a woman's voice! It was the same woman! Tiger knew it was the same woman!

Chapter 8

The missing drum

"I wonder what he's doing?" said Sam, as he and Kerry waited for Mr Crompton to return to his office.

"Give him a chance," said Kerry and she stepped forwards towards Mr Crompton's desk and picked up a glass paperweight that had caught her attention. She drew the paperweight towards her eyes and stared into its depths. "He's only been out of the room half a minute."

Then Kerry's heart missed a beat, for there in front of her on the desk, was a memo pad. As she stared through the paperweight, the printed name at the top of the pad became magnified so that it seemed to leap out at her. Kerry's mouth fell open. She lowered the paperweight and checked the memo pad with her own eyes. There was no mistake. She grabbed Sam's arm and pointed with her free hand. She did not speak.

"What's the matter?" said Sam.

He had caught sight of Kerry's face, drained of colour, deathly pale, as if she had seen a ghost.

"The pad!" stammered Kerry. "The name on the pad! What does it mean, Sam?"

Sam followed her gaze until his eyes settled on the small, rectangular memo pad and there, in blue print on the top sheet, was printed the name 'Tetrochem Ltd'.

Sam reached forward and picked the pad up as if to check that it really did exist.

"It says 'Tetrochem Ltd'," said Sam slowly. "Crompton must know the firm."

"Look in his desk," said Kerry, regaining her senses. "Quickly, before he gets back."

Sam pulled opn the top drawer of Mr Crompton's desk. He rummaged around for a moment and then withdrew a letter, hand written and signed by Mr Crompton. Once again, proudly displayed at the top of the page was the firm's name and address 'Tetrochem Ltd, Blackshaw'.

"He's coming back!" said Kerry. "Give it to me, quick!"

Kerry folded the letter and shoved it in the inside pocket of her jacket. Sam leaned back against the desk and pushed the drawer closed with his left hand as Mr Crompton re-entered the room.

"Right!" he said, clapping his hands together. "Jonathan Crompton's ready for action. Let's get going, shall we?"

Sam hesitated and then said, "I … er, I think we'd better get back to school if you don't mind. We'll leave the police to you."

"Nonsense!" said Mr Crompton, his moustache beginning to twitch again. "I won't hear of it! You must come with me to the police station. I really do insist. The police will want to talk to you. I'm certain of that."

"But we're missing school," began Kerry. "We really must get back."

"I've told you, I won't hear of it," repeated Mr Crompton, and he stepped forward and took hold of Kerry's arm. "Believe me, I know what I'm doing. I'll speak to your head teacher and tell her how sensibly you have both acted. Don't forget, I'm holding a meeting at your school this evening. Your head teacher is sure to be attending. I promise you I'll have a word with her this evening. How does that sound?"

"All right," said Sam, glancing at his sister's worried face. "It sounds fine."

"Good. That's settled, then," said Mr Crompton. "Let's not waste any more time, eh?"

Mr Crompton led the children out of the room, his hand still holding on to Kerry's arm.

As they approached Mr Crompton's black BMW, Sam half-thought of making a run for it but that would mean leaving his sister behind and he quickly rejected the idea. No, they would have to sit it out in the car and hope that an opportunity would arise for them to escape.

Sam and Kerry climbed into the back of the car and it was not long before they were speeding along Thicketford Road back towards Blackshaw.

"I must just call at my works office on the way," said Mr Crompton. "Some papers I need urgently. You don't mind, do you?"

Sam and Kerry did not reply. They exchanged frightened glances and sat back in the car. There was absolutely nothing they could do. Mr Crompton was in full control.

Five minutes later, the BMW drove through the gates of Tetrochem Ltd. A huge wooden board was placed near the entrance with the words CLOSED DOWN painted roughly on it in red. Mr Crompton cruised into the yard and brought the car to a stop as Jacko approached.

Crompton switched off the engine, glanced in the rear view mirror and said, "You'd better get out."

"What are we doing here?" said Kerry, although she felt she already knew the answer.

"Just get out," snapped Crompton. His voice had changed. It was cold and hard.

Jacko opened the back door of the car and Sam and Kerry shuffled out. Jacko immediately gripped Sam by the back of the collar, a strong firm grip that almost lifted him off his feet.

"Don't even think of making a run for it," threatened Jacko.

"Take them to the office," ordered Crompton. "I need to speak to Kim."

Sam was half pushed, half carried across the yard towards a brick building with a green door. Kerry followed, with Mr Crompton giving her a gentle push as if to remind her he was still there.

Inside the office, a woman with short, black hair was sitting behind a large wooden desk. A smaller, dark-haired man was standing near the window. He glared at the children as they entered.

Kim stood up and banged her hand down on the desk.

"What a mess!" she said, as Crompton came through the door and shut it behind him. "What a mess you've got us into!"

"Shut up!" snapped Crompton. "There's no mess. Everything's all right."

"No mess?" stormed Kim and she banged her hand down again. "Everything's all right, is it?" Don't make me laugh!" Then she turned to Jacko and said, "Tell him, Jacko."

"We can't find one of the drums," said Jacko. "There's one missing. We've searched all around the quarry and we can't find it."

The colour visibly drained from Mr Crompton's face. He stuttered for a moment and then said, "What do you mean you can't find it? That drum is down there somewhere. You get back and you find it! I don't care how long it takes – you find it!"

"Yes, Mr Crompton," said Jacko and he signalled to his friend and backed out of the room.

"It was a stupid idea," said Kim. "Jacko should never have dumped them there in the first place. It was too close to home."

"We've got away with it before," snapped Mr Crompton. "Don't tell me you've got a conscience all of a sudden? You know very well we had to get rid of them before the inspectors arrived. It's never bothered you in the past."

"It was too close to home," repeated Kim. "We've never dumped so close to home before. And what are we going to do about these two?" She nodded towards Sam and Kerry.

"They're not a problem" said Mr Crompton. "We keep them until everything's cleared up; until we're sure the quarry's clean. They're only kids. No one is going to believe a word they say – especially if they haven't got a scrap of evidence to back up their story."

"You've forgotten about Tiger," said Kerry. "He's probably at the police station right now. You'll have to let us go."

For the first time, Kim smiled. She turned to face Crompton and said, "You don't need to worry about the other one. Come with me – I'll show you."

Vetch and his friends just could not keep away from the quarry. They were attracted to the heap of rubbish like flies. It was the environment they felt most at home in.

"You can find all sorts of things on rubbish tips," said Ginger, scraping at the heap with his hands. "I found a wallet once on the town tip. It had a fiver inside. I've still got the wallet at home."

"Shows how useful tips are then, doesn't it?" said Vetch. He had a metal bar in his hand and was thrashing at a huge hawthorn bush. "Nothing wrong with tipping rubbish is there? It's useful."

"Yeah," said Kaz. "Rubbish can be really useful."

"There's an old scarf up here," said Ginger, pulling at one end of a red and white football scarf. "I don't know why somebody's thrown that away. It's a bit dirty and it smells a little but it would be all right after a wash."

He picked it out of the heap and wrapped it around his neck.

"Nothing wrong with that," said Kaz. "It suits you, Ginger."

There was a sudden metallic clang as Vetch's metal bar made contact with something concealed beneath the hawthorn bush. He stood back and prodded the bush with his bar.

"There's something under here! Come and give us a hand, will you?"

Ginger jumped down from the rubbish heap, the red and white scarf still wound round his neck, and he and Kaz joined Vetch near the hawthorn bush.

"It's a container of some kind," said Vetch, peering through the branches. "A great metal drum. Give me a hand to get it out, will you. It could be worth a bit."

Kaz and Ginger stepped forward and the three of

them took a grip on the drum.

"Pull it!" shouted Vetch. "It'll roll if you give a good pull!"

They took the strain and heaved upwards and, sure enough, the metal drum rolled forward clear of the hawthorn bush.

"Ugh! It's leaking," said Ginger. "I've got it on my hands."

A thick brown paste was oozing from the container and both Vetch and Ginger had made contact with it.

"What is it?" said Kaz. "It's nothing harmful, is it?"

"Of course it's nothing harmful," said Vetch and he rubbed his hands on his trousers to try to get rid of the sticky brown mess.

"Vetch … it's stinging me!" said Ginger. "My hands are hurting!"

"Don't be so soft," said Vetch and, without thinking, he instinctively raised a hand and rubbed his eye.

The effect was instant. Vetch let out a scream that grew and echoed around the empty quarry. He rubbed at his eyes and screamed again, dropping on to his knees with the pain.

"What's wrong with him?" shouted Kaz. "What's wrong with him, Ginger?"

Ginger ignored her. He was shaking his hands and rubbing them on his clothes.

"They're burning," he said, a look of fear in his wide eyes. You've got to help me, Kaz! My hands are burning!"

Kaz looked at Vetch and then at Ginger and then back

to Vetch again. She didn't know what to do. Then she made up her mind. She turned and ran. She ran out of the quarry as fast as she could and Vetch's screams followed her; followed her up the track at the side of the quarry; followed her on to the top road where she raced towards an oncoming car, waving her hands frantically, forcing the driver to jam on his brakes and screech to a halt near the frightened, hysterical girl.

—Chapter 9—
Tiger takes control

It took Tiger two hours to work the rope loose. Jacko had picked him up and thrown him on to the back of the truck. He was bruised and battered but fairly certain that no bones had been broken. Jacko had pulled the rope tight so that it cut into Tiger's wrists and the more he wriggled his hands and worked his fingers, the more the rope bit into his skin.

To make matters worse, the rope was tied to the back of the driver's cab, which meant that Tiger's arms were pulled backwards above his head. Nevertheless, Tiger had persevered and now, two hours after being trussed up like a Christmas turkey, the rope was loose and he could make his escape. Tiger gave one last twist and pulled his hands downwards. His face contorted in pain as the rope grated and scraped but then his left hand broke free. He eased the rope over his other hand and his arms dropped like lead weights.

Tiger could not move for a moment. He just sat on the back of the vehicle, head bowed, breathing heavily. His wrists hurt and throbbed but he was loose.

"I've got to get out of here," he said to himself and he scrambled down from the back of the truck.

He looked around. It was no use wasting time on the up-and-over door. He had already tried that route and it had led to disaster. No, there must be another way.

Tiger wandered towards the back of the building where he had noticed the other parked vehicles and, as he rounded a pile of boxes, stacked precariously on top of each other, he let out a low whistle. He had recognised one of the vehicles. There were two vans, both with the firm's name painted on the side but, parked in between them, was a maroon hatchback – the very same maroon hatchback that Tiger had seen parked on double yellow lines outside the Blackshaw Building Society.

"Now I'm sure it's her," said Tiger. He was muttering to himself, scratching his chin, staring at the maroon car. "They're not only polluting the area, they're robbing it as well!"

Tiger approached the car. He tried the handle and was surprised to find that the door opened at once. He looked inside and there, discarded on the back seat, was a khaki army hat and a pair of dark glasses.

"I'll have those for evidence," said Tiger and he reached across and grabbed the items, shoving them inside his jacket and pulling up the zip.

Tiger closed the car door and looked around again. It was then that he saw the door. It was only a very small door, set into the back of the storage building and so small that a man of Jacko's size would have to bend down to enter, but it was still a door and it offered Tiger hope of escape. He hurried towards it, praying that it was not locked. He seized the handle, turned it and pulled. The door did not budge. It was firm and fast and no matter how hard Tiger pulled and tugged at the handle it would not give way.

"Blast it!" said Tiger and then looked round guiltily in case someone had heard him. "What's the use of having a door if I can't get out of it!"

Tiger stepped forward again and examined the door more closely. It was wooden and it seemed to be made up of two panels. The bottom section looked as if it had been recently repaired and whoever had undertaken the work had not made a particularly good job of it.

"It looks loose," said Tiger, pushing against the panel. "It'll give way with a good belt."

He stood back, steadied himself and then took a flying leap towards the door, hitting the bottom panel full on with both feet. There was a cracking sound and a stabbing pain shot up Tiger's right leg. He crashed to the floor, landing flat on his back. The door juddered and shook but looked as secure as ever.

"Forget that," said Tiger from his position on the floor. "I'm going to do myself an injury."

He stood up and glared with hate at the door. "If only there was something I could batter it with, I'm sure it would give way."

Then he stopped, almost frozen to the spot for a moment. A picture had flashed into his mind, an idea which, if it worked would offer him a way to break out of the storage shed.

"It's worth a try," said Tiger and he turned away from the door and headed back into the storage unit.

He went straight towards the up-and-over door and, when he got there, he stopped and turned – and there was the fork-lift truck, parked to the left of the door, its steel forks at ground level beneath a rough, wooden platform.

"Just the job!" said Tiger, rubbing his hands together. "This is just what I need!"

"They've got Tiger," said Kerry, her voice quivering more with anger than with fear. "I know they have. What are we going to do?"

"We're going to get out," said Sam, irritably. "I don't plan to stay locked up in this office for the rest of my life."

"Oh great," said Kerry. "Trouble is the door's locked and what's more there's a huge metal grating on the window."

"I can see that," said Sam, "but there must be a way."

"Of course there is," said Kerry, staring down at the office desk. "The phone! We can ring the police!"

"Brilliant!" said Sam and made a grab for the red, push-button phone that rested on top of the desk.

Sam lifted the receiver and pushed the number nine button three times. He put the receiver to his ear and listened. Nothing. The phone was absolutely dead. Sam threw down the receiver in frustration.

"You can tell this place has closed down," said Kerry. "This isn't a working office. There are no letters or documents lying around and everywhere's dusty."

"You're right," said Sam. "That's why the phone's been cut off."

"We're stuck, then," said Kerry. "We'll just have to sit it out and hope that somebody misses us."

"I wonder what Tiger would do if he was here?" said Sam. "Tiger would have a plan. He wouldn't just sit it out."

Tiger climbed on to the moulded plastic seat and looked at the controls in front of him. It looked simple enough. There was a red starter button and a small lever on the panel. Tiger guessed that this was for forward and reverse. A second lever was marked 'raise' and 'lower' so there was no mistaking that this worked the fork.

"If I take it steady I'll be all right," said Tiger and he put his finger on the red starter button and pressed it down gently. There was a click, a whirring sound and the motor purred into life. Tiger remembered that he had to press down the clutch pedal before engaging the gear and he glanced down at the floor. He rested his left foot on the plate and pressed. At the same time, he pulled back the gear lever.

"Now – gently does it … "

Tiger gradually released the clutch and the fork-lift truck moved slowly backwards until the fork was clear of the wooden platform.

"Easy," said Tiger, as he brought the truck to a halt. "I'm going to enjoy this!"

For the next five minutes, Tiger experimented. He raised and lowered the fork, he turned the truck, he moved it backwards and forwards and he stopped it at will. Only once did he misjudge the steering and career into a stack of boxes, sending them crashing to the floor. All things considered, Tiger felt pretty pleased with himself.

He drove the fork-lift past the truck, past the vans and the maroon getaway car and then brought it to a halt. He thought for a moment and then reached inside his jacket and pulled out the khaki army hat and dark glasses he had taken from the car.

"I'll wear these. Just the thing for battle." He placed the hat on his head and fixed the glasses in position on his nose. "Right," he said, setting the fork at the desired height. "Now for that door!"

Tiger slammed the gear lever into forward, lowered his head and charged like an angry rhino. There was a

crashing, splintering sound as the fork-lift truck hit its target and tore the door completely from its hinges. Tiger broke through the gap and trundled out into the works yard. He brought the truck to a stop and glanced around anxiously. There was no sign of anyone. The yard was completely deserted. The very next moment, Tiger heard the most strange sound and it seemed to be coming from a separate building on the far side of the yard. There were voices shouting and then there was banging on the door as if someone was trying to attract his attention.

Tiger jumped down from the fork-lift truck and moved cautiously towards the building. He recognised those voices! Tiger stepped up to the window, cupped his hands and stared through the metal grating. He stepped back quickly, his eyes wide with amazement.

"Sam! Kerry!" he muttered and then he banged on the metal grating and shouted their names.

Sam's face appeared at the window and Tiger said, "What are you doing in there?"

"Well, we're not having a party, are we?" said Sam. "Get us out, will you."

"Do you like my disguise?" said Tiger, raising his glasses. "Pretty good, eh?"

"Brilliant," said Sam. "We hardly recognised you. Now will you get us out of here!"

Tiger tried the door and said, "Sam – the door's locked."

There was a pause before an angry voice replied, "Of course it's locked, stupid. If it wasn't locked we would have left hours ago!"

"I see," said Tiger thoughtfully. "Just hang on a minute. I'll break it down with my fork-lift truck. Get to the back of the room."

Sam and Kerry moved away from the door and crouched down behind the desk at the far side of the room. The next moment there was an almighty crash and the door seemed to be coming in towards them before it split apart to reveal Tiger sitting triumphantly in the driver's seat of the fork-lift truck, a broad grin on his face.

"I've always wanted to drive one of these," said Tiger, jumping down from the truck. "Listen, you know that robbery at the building society? You'll never guess what I've found out ...", and he proceeded to tell Sam and Kerry all about the maroon getaway car and the woman driver.

" ... and this is her hat and these are her glasses," concluded Tiger. "Suit me, don't they?"

"We've got to get out of here," said Sam, "before they come back to check us."

He had no sooner spoken than the sound of a car could be heard pulling up outside.

"They're coming," shouted Kerry, rushing towards the door. "We should have run for it! There's someone coming!"

"We're trapped," said Sam. "There's only one way out and we're trapped!"

—Chapter 10—
Escape

"Get on the back of the truck," said Tiger, jumping up into the driver's seat. "I'm not getting caught again!"

Sam and Kerry jumped on to a metal footplate at the back of the truck and held on for all they were worth as Tiger pressed the starter button and brought the fork-lift truck back to life. He pulled down on the steering wheel and the truck spun round to face the open office doorway.

"Hang on!" shouted Tiger and he pressed the accelerator flat to the floor.

The fork-lift truck shot forward out of the office into the gathering gloom of the early evening. In the factory yard, Kim and Jacko were just about to get out of a light-blue Metro Kim had been driving. She had turned off the engine, opened the door and put one foot out of the car when she stopped still and stared with amazement as a fork-lift truck appeared to be charging straight in her direction.

Jacko's mouth dropped open as he caught sight of Tiger at the wheel, his khaki hat and glasses making him look like some sort of avenging mercenary. He pointed a finger at the truck and said, "It's going to hit us, Kim! That crazy kid is going to hit us!"

Kim reacted quickly. She slammed the door shut,

started the engine and jerked the gear stick into reverse. It was too late. Tiger was on to them. The steel fork thudded into the body of the Metro, sending it reeling sideways. Tiger let out a yell of satisfaction and reached for the lever that operated the fork. He jerked it backwards and the fork began to rise, lifting Jacko's side

of the car completely off the ground. Jacko looked terrified. His eyes bulged and his face turned red. The car tottered for a moment, then rolled and tumbled, first on to its side and then over again on to its roof. Tiger let out another yell, backed away and then drove the fork-lift truck towards the open factory gates.

"We've done it!" shouted Sam from the footplate. "Let's go!"

Once outside the gates, the children jumped from the fork-lift truck and ran for all they were worth.

It took them forty-five minutes to get back to Blackshaw. They had decided to head straight for the police station. By the time they got there the sun had completely disappeared, dark clouds were building and gathering, tumbling in from the moors and spilling over the town. It was getting distinctly colder.

"I know them in here," said Tiger, as he stood in the entrance. He had removed his dark glasses but he was still wearing the khaki army hat. "I came here after the building society robbery."

Tiger led the way through the double doors and the children found themselves facing a long counter. An angry-looking lady wearing a thick tweed coat was shouting at a policeman who had a harassed expression on his face. The lady's husband, a small, insignificant-looking man, who looked as though he needed a good meal, stood meekly to one side.

Tiger surveyed the situation and made his decision.

"This is urgent," he said. "I don't think she'll mind me interrupting."

He strode up to the counter, coughed loudly and said, "Excuse me. I'm sorry to interrupt but I need to talk to someone right away."

There was a moment's silence as the lady caught her breath. She looked at the policeman, she looked at her husband, she put her hands on her hips and then she said, "That's just typical! Now you see what I mean, officer! This is an example of the sort of youth that is hanging around outside my house causing noise and disturbance."

Tiger looked puzzled.

"No manners, you see! No manners and too much money to spend!"

"I'm sorry to interrupt," repeated Tiger, politely, "but this really is very important."

"Don't I know you?" said the policeman from behind the counter. "Haven't I seen you before?"

"Yes," said Tiger. "At the Blackshaw Building Society. I witnessed the robbery."

"That's right," said the policeman, breaking into a smile. "A very good witness, too, as I recall. It's Tahir, isn't it? What can I do for you young man?"

"Well really!" stormed the lady in the tweed coat. "This is intolerable! I was in the middle of making a complaint, you know. You haven't heard the last of this! Mark my words, young man, you haven't heard the last of this!"

And with that she beckoned to her husband and stamped out of the station.

Tiger looked at his friends and then said,

"I'm sorry to cause trouble but I've got to speak to Inspector Fairhurst?"

"We haven't got much time," butted in Kerry. "If we're not quick, Kim and Jacko will warn him and he'll get away."

The officer looked puzzled. "Who'll get away?" he said. "What are you talking about?"

"Mr Crompton," said Kerry. "He's involved in the building society robbery. He's a director of Tetrochem and that's the firm that polluted the river. All his posters say how he really cares … and he doesn't care at all. He's a crook!"

"Now just you hold on a minute, young lady," began the officer. "If you mean Jonathan Crompton, you can't go accusing a respectable gentleman like that without some proof. He's standing in the elections, you know. I really don't think he'd be stupid enough to get involved in a building society robbery, do you?"

"Please can I see Inspector Fairhurst," repeated Tiger. "He'd listen to me. I'm sure he would."

The police officer began to look uncomfortable. "Inspector Fairhurst is off duty. He's not in the station and there's no way I'm going to contact him with a cock and bull story about Mr Crompton. It would be more than my job's worth."

"We're wasting time," said Kerry, and she slapped her arms against her sides in exasperation. "Don't you understand, he's going to get away! They're all going to get away!"

"Pass me the letter," said Sam and he held his hand out towards his sister.

Kerry reached inside her jacket and pulled out the letterhead she had taken from Mr Cromton's desk. She passed it across to her brother.

"Look," he said, waving it at the policeman. "Mr Crompton's name's on the top of this and Tetrochem have been dumping chemical drums in the quarry. They've poisoned the local river. You've got to do something."

The policeman took the letterhead, studied it for a moment and then said, "All right, come back tomorrow, eh, and I'll see if the inspector will have a word with you."

"Oh! This is hopeless!" shouted Kerry. "They're going to get away! If you won't do something then I will!"

She turned and ran out of the police station as the startled officer stared after her, open-mouthed.

"Look, we've been held prisoner by these people," said Tiger. "They tied me to a truck. If you don't believe me, look at my wrists."

Tiger extended his hands, palms upwards, towards the police officer, whose eyes widened and who gave a gasp of amazement as he stared at the boy's wrists. They were bruised and red-raw where the ropes had pulled and bitten into the flesh.

At the same moment the telephone rang and the officer instinctively reached out to answer it.

"Blackshaw Police Station," he barked. "How can I

help you?" There was a pause and then he said, "Missing children? How many of them? Three, you say? Don't worry, Mrs Simpson, I've got a feeling I know exactly where they are. No, you stay there at home. They're quite safe. There are just one or two matters we need to clear up. Now don't worry. They'll be brought back to you." The officer put the receiver down.

Tiger reached in his pocket and took out the dark glasses. "This hat and these glasses," he said, placing them on the counter, "were worn by Kim, the driver of the getaway car in the robbery. You'll need those as evidence, won't you?"

Sam stepped forward and said, "You told my mum that we were all safe but we're not all here, are we? My sister was here but she's disappeared, hasn't she? That's because you wouldn't believe her, would you?"

The policeman looked uncomfortable. He shuffled around for a moment and then he raised a wooden counter that separated him from the boys.

"You'd better come through to an interview room," he said, beckoning them forward. "I think I'd better bring Inspector Fairhurst in on this one."

Outside, in the pressing gloom, the first giant spots of rain were beginning to fall from a sky that threatened an onslaught. Kerry was wearing only a light jacket and she pulled the collar up and set off away from the police station at a brisk pace. She checked her watch and nodded with satisfaction. She still had time, plenty of time. Mr Crompton would only just be starting his speech.

— Chapter 11 —
The final curtain

By the time Kerry had reached Pebble Street School, the rain was driving down on her and still getting heavier. The sky was rumbling like an angry giant and, as Kerry passed between the rows of parked cars, there was a vicious flash that lit the night and made the old school stand out in ghostly silhouette. Kerry stopped abrubtly and rested a hand against the nearest car, then, as she glanced down, she realised that it was Mr Crompton's car, the same black BMW that had carried her as a prisoner to the Tetrochem factory. Parked directly behind the BMW was a strange-looking, vivid orange car that caught Kerry's attention and looked vaguely familiar. The flash was over in an instant, the noise subsided and Kerry moved on.

She entered the school yard, advanced towards the door, pushed it open and stepped inside. She stood for a moment in the narrow entrance, soaked to the skin, water pouring off her and forming a spreading puddle on the cold stone floor. A short corridor led to the hall and, as Kerry moved forward, she could hear Crompton's voice over the microphone, loud and clear, confidently addressing his audience.

Kerry eased her way through the swing doors and stood in the semi-darkness at the back of the hall.

Crompton was in full flow. He was standing behind a wooden table placed at the very front of the stage, which was brightly lit in contrast to the rest of the hall.

" ... and if you care about the environment," pronounced Mr Crompton, "then my party is the only party to vote for. If you want a clean town, a town fit to live in ... "

Kerry glanced around and spotted a spare seat. She moved forward and took her place quietly. No sooner had she sat down than she felt a dig in her ribs and, when she glanced to her right, she saw that it was Gary, her mum's hairdresser. Of course – the old orange car! There was only one car like that in the whole of Blackshaw. Gary nodded towards Mr Crompton on the stage and raised his thumb in approval.

"You were right," whispered Gary. "Mr Crompton really does care. It was you who convinced me to come and listen to him."

Kerry looked the other way and it was then that she noticed Kim and Jacko. They were standing at the far side of the hall, leaning against the wall, staring towards the stage. It was as if they were waiting for Crompton to finish his speech to give him some sort of signal, some sort of warning.

"And if you care for the future of your children," implored Mr Crompton, spreading his arms like a protecting angel, "then there can be only one candidate to vote for. Vote for Jonathan Crompton and remember what I say to you – Jonathan Crompton really cares."

Mr Crompton sat down and at once there was a spontaneous burst of applause, supported by loud cheers from the front of the hall. Mr Crompton milked the applause, smiling and bowing and raising an arm in salute.

Kerry remained unmoved, her wet clothes steaming steadily in the hall's warmth.

Eventually, the applause subsided and Mr Crompton sat down and sipped at a glass of water. A large lady to Mr Crompton's left stood up and approached the microphone. She coughed twice and said, "I'm sure you'll agree with me when I say that was a wonderful speech."

The audience murmured its approval.

"Jonathan Crompton has inspired us all to work for a better environment. Mr Crompton has indicated that he is willing to accept any questions, so if you have anything to ask now is the time to put it to our candidate."

The large lady sat down again and scanned the audience. Nobody spoke and she was just about to get to her feet again when Kerry stood up.

"I've got a question for Mr Crompton," she said, and two hundred heads turned to see where the voice was coming from. "I'd like to ask Mr Crompton if he knows about a firm called Tetrochem?"

Crompton looked uneasy. He shuffled in his seat and the smile disappeared from his face. He rose slowly to his feet and said, "As a matter of fact I do know about Tetrochem and I have been saddened to hear that the firm is to close due to financial difficulties. I have been very proud to serve as a director of this long-established firm. Over the years the company has provided many jobs for the people of Blackshaw and the closure will be a great blow to the community. Now, if there are any other questions?"

Kerry would not let the matter drop.

"Are you proud to be connected with a firm that illegally dumps chemicals, Mr Crompton?"

There was a gasp from the audience. Gary pulled at Kerry's sleeve but she shook him off. Kim and Jacko were moving towards her along the narrow gap behind the people at the back of the hall.

"Are you proud to be connected with a firm that dumps dangerous chemicals in a local quarry and then tries to cover it up when the drums leak into a stream and pollute the river?"

"This is outrageous!" stormed Mr Crompton from the front of the stage. "There is no foundation to these allegations! I demand an apology!"

"Do you believe in keeping young children prisoners?" shouted Kerry. She was beginning to enjoy herself. "And do you know anything about a robbery at Blackshaw Building Society?"

"Enough!" shouted Mr Crompton, slamming his hand down on the wooden table. "I don't know what you're talking about. This really is enough!"

The room was in chaos. People had jumped to their feet and someone had switched the hall lights on. Gary was tugging at Kerry's arm but still she would not sit down.

The doors at the back of the hall burst open and three burly policemen appeared in the gap. Joanathan Crompton took one look at them and made a dash for the back of the stage.

"Come on!" said Kerry. "He's escaping! Don't let him get away!"

She dragged Gary from his seat and the two of them forced their way through the chaotic crowd. They reached the gap at the back of the hall and there, straight in front of them, were Kim and Jacko, staring at the policemen who confronted them.

"That's them!" shouted a familiar voice and Tiger's face appeared between two of the policemen.

"They're the ones!" shouted Sam, pushing his way forward and pointing towards Kim and Jacko.

The policemen moved forward as Kim and Jacko leapt over the nearest row of seats in an attempt to make their escape.

"Leave them to it," said Kerry, dragging Gary towards the exit.

They left the chaos of the school hall and rushed out into the torrential Blackshaw rain.

"What on earth's going on?" shouted Gary as the rain drove into his face.

"Follow me," said Kerry. "I know where his car is."

They ran through the pounding rain towards the rows of parked cars and, as they staggered through the school gates, they were just in time to hear the black BMW roar into life and see the headlights blaze through the rain and the wheels spin as Mr Crompton screamed up the street away from the school.

Kerry turned to Gary in frustration. "Follow him!" she shouted. "He mustn't get away!"

"No problem," said Gary and he raced to the door of his orange Ford.

As soon as he was in, he turned the key in the ignition and prepared for action. The engine coughed, spluttered, coughed again and died.

"Gary!" yelled Kerry in anguish. "What sort of a car is this!"

"It'll be fine," said Gary, turning the key again. "I tuned it up myself. It just doesn't like the damp."

Crompton's BMW was already turning the corner at the top of the road. The rain beat down relentlessly, battering on to the front windscreen.

"Come on," coaxed Gary, as the engine moaned and stuttered. "Come on, please!"

The engine fired and grew and burst into life.

"Great!" said Gary, as he thrust the lever into first gear. "It doesn't like the damp. I have to use my hairdrier on it sometimes. Let's go!"

The car leapt forward, the wheels spinning viciously, sending a spray of dirty water spurting in all directions.

"He's got a good lead on us," said Kerry. "Do you think we'll catch him?"

"Course we will," said Gary, confidently. "There's

really only one way he can go. With a bit of luck he'll be held up at the lights on the crossroads."

Gary was right. As they raced past the market place and approached the crossroads, Crompton's BMW could be seen, raring to get away at the traffic lights.

The rain drove down heavier still. It was a huge cloudburst.

The traffic lights changed and Crompton's BMW roared off, the wheels screaming and steaming on the soaked surface. Gary's car chugged after him, the speedometer straining to reach 50 mph.

"Can't you go any quicker?" urged Kerry.

Gary looked insulted and jammed his foot down to the floor. "He's taking the road out of Blackshaw past the quarry," he said. "He could do with slowing down in these conditions."

The BMW powered on, pulling away with every second that passed. Kerry was vaguely aware of a blue flashing light and a police siren sounding somewhere behind her but her eyes were glued to the front, straining through the rain and the darkness, fixed on the red tail lights at the back of Mr Crompton's car.

Then the strangest thing happened. The BMW seemed to swerve and veer from the road. It went to the right and to the left and then it seemed to soar upwards for a moment, slowing down at the same time.

Gary's eyes widened in horror.

"He's missed the bend!" he screamed. "He's missed the turn in the road! He's gone off into the quarry!"

Crompton's black BMW seemed to hang in mid-air, frozen in the yellow beam from Gary's headlights. The front of the car dipped and then it plummeted from view, leaving nothing but cold, empty darkness that was immediately filled by the driving rain.

"He's gone over the edge!" repeated Gary, as the orange Ford stopped at the brink of the quarry. "Crompton's gone over the edge!"

Gary flung open the driver's door and raced out into the rain. Kerry followed at once and the two of them stood at the edge of the quarry and stared down into its depths.

Kerry's brain was pounding. The yellow headlights from Gary's car cut through the rain and traversed the quarry. The police siren that had been vaguely present inside Kerry's head grew louder and louder and then trailed away in a confused wailing of flashing blue light. A car door slammed and Kerry was aware of figures approaching from the rear. She felt a hand on her arm and when she turned she saw that it was Sam.

"Are you all right?" said Sam.

Tiger was standing a few paces behind him.

"I'm all right," said Kerry slowly.

Another police car pulled up behind the first one.

"He's gone over the edge," said Gary. "He missed the bend and he's gone over the edge."

A policeman stepped forward and shone a powerful torch down into the quarry. The yellow-white beam searched through the rain for a moment and then settled on a heap of crumpled, smoking metal that had been Crompton's BMW.

"I've got it!" said the officer and he had no sooner spoken than a terrific explosion ripped through the night sky.

"Get back!" shouted the policeman and another explosion erupted immediately, tearing into the darkness, illuminating the quarry.

The figures at the edge of the precipice had raced for the cover of the cars and only when one of the policemen signalled to them that it was safe did they venture forward.

They moved to the edge of the path overlooking the quarry and stared down at what was left of the burning wreckage. As they stared into the depths of the quarry, a figure became visible, staggering around like a drunken man some distance away from the wreckage.

It was Tiger who spotted it first. He grabbed hold of Sam's arm, pointed into the quarry and said, "Look! There's something moving! He's alive!"

The policeman shone his beam towards the figure. Crompton tottered forward, reached a hand out in front of him towards the light and then collapsed to the ground in a crumpled heap.

The policeman turned off his torch.

The rain beat down relentlessly.

—Chapter 12—

Seeing the light

It was Monday morning. Tiger, Sam and Kerry had needed a few days to recover from their ordeal and it was their first day back at school. The sky was clear and bright and spring blue and the storm that had struck Blackshaw with such force was no more than a memory.

Mrs Wilson had seen the children arriving through the school gate and, although it was only a quarter to nine, she had wanted to talk to them, so had asked them up to her classroom.

"I feel awful," said Mrs Wilson. "You told me your suspicions about the river being polluted and I did nothing about it. I promised to make some enquiries and then other things just seemed to take over. I suppose my mind has been on our own conservation area. I feel very guilty."

"It's not your fault," said Tiger. "We thought we were safe going to Mr Crompton for help. After all, he was campaigning for a cleaner environment."

"I can't believe Tetrochem was involved in illegal chemical dumping," said Mrs Wilson. "Over the years, it's been one of the most respected firms in Blackshaw. My own father worked there! And Mr Crompton – to think I was going to vote for him in the elections!"

"Inspector Fairhurst told us that Crompton got

himself deeper and deeper into trouble," said Sam. "Apparently, he'd put a lot of money into Tetrochem some years ago and then things started to go wrong with the firm."

"Inspector Fairhurst said it had been managed badly," interrupted Kerry.

"They started cutting corners on safety regulations and that's when the illegal dumping began," said Sam.

"They got away with it at first," said Tiger. "They took the drums well away from Blackshaw and made sure they couldn't be traced back to Tetrochem. But then inspectors visited the factory and demanded safety improvements. The firm just couldn't afford to pay for them and that's when it closed down."

"But why did they dump drums in the quarry?" asked Mrs Wilson. "Surely they knew that the drums would be discovered – and they must have realised that the police would suspect Tetrochem. After all, it is – or was – the only chemical firm in the area."

"We don't know why they used the quarry," said Kerry. "Inspector Fairhurst thinks Jacko – that's the man who drove the truck – just couldn't be bothered to drive a long way from Blackshaw."

"I think Kim and Jacko had their minds on other things," said Sam. "It was them who robbed the building society. Mr Crompton knew nothing about it."

"They were going to lose their jobs, you see," explained Kerry.

"Everything was going well," said Sam, "until Tiger turned up."

"It's amazing," said Mrs Wilson, rising from her desk. "And what about Mr Crompton? I believe he came to grief in the very quarry where the chemicals had been dumped?"

"He lost control of his car in the storm," said Kerry. "It was terrible. He went right over the edge and then the car exploded."

"He's lucky to be alive," said Sam. "He's in a serious condition but he's expected to survive. He's in Blackshaw Hospital."

"He'll never get elected now, though," said Tiger. "Kim and Jacko have blamed him for dumping the drums and the police have searched Crompton's house and recovered Sam's film from the desk in his office. They've got all the evidence they need."

"Terrible business, all of it," said Mrs Wilson, "but I must say you children come out of it with great credit. Pebble Street is very proud of you. However, it is nearly nine o'clock, the bell is about to go and it's back to work as usual. What do you say to that?"

"Terrific," said Tiger, pulling a face. "We really can't wait!"

Monday afternoon saw Mrs Wilson's class working in the conservation area. Much of the damage had been repaired but there was still plenty of work to be done.

Tiger and Sam were given a piece of ground to hoe and loosen up in readiness for planting vegetables. It was a little early for planting as yet but Mrs Wilson had explained that the ground needed plenty of preparation. As they worked in the warm, afternoon sunshine, the events of the previous few days seemed to drift into insignificance. It was only when a sharp, rasping voice disturbed their concentration that the boys were brought back to reality.

The boys turned to face the voice and saw that it was Ginger, sitting astride the stone wall, his arms folded, his hands bandaged.

"Hey, you two! Come over here a minute, will you!"

Sam and Tiger looked at each other. They dropped their garden tools and wandered over towards Ginger.

"What do you want?" said Tiger, staring up at the older boy. "Come to gloat again, have you?"

Kaz's face appeared above the wall. She pulled herself up to sit by Ginger.

"Have you heard what happened to Vetch?" said Kaz. "Do you know what happened down at the quarry?"

Sam and Tiger looked puzzled. "We haven't heard anything," said Sam. "We've been a bit busy for the last few days."

"You'd better have a look, then," said Kaz and she and Ginger both reached a hand down on the other side of the wall.

In an instant, Vetch appeared beside them. He was wearing dark glasses and his face was even more red and blotched than usual. Like Ginger, his hands were swathed in bandages.

"What's the matter with you?" said Tiger. "You look as

though you've been in a fight."

"I wish I had," said Vetch. His voice was quieter than usual, more subdued. "As a matter of fact, I've been in the hospital. We were messing around down in the quarry. We found a great metal drum and when we tried to move it we realised it was leaking some chemical. I got the stuff all over my hands and in my eyes. I've never known anything like it. I felt as though my eyes were burning out."

"You should have heard him scream," chipped in Kaz. "I've never heard anyone scream like Vetch did."

"They rushed me off to hospital," continued Vetch. "Kept me in overnight. They kept washing and bathing my eyes and they put a dressing over them. They thought I was going to lose the sight in my left eye but it seems as if it should heal all right now. I never want to go through that again."

"I'm sorry," said Sam sincerely. "It must have been awful."

"It was my own fault," said Vetch. He took his glasses off and squinted in the strong sunshine. His eyes were bloodshot and watery. "The thing is, I've learnt my lesson. It was like a message."

"Vetch thinks he's been given a message," asserted Ginger.

"It's you who were right," continued Vetch. "What you're doing, I mean. Trying to protect the environment, trying to tidy things up."

"Keep it clean!" said Tiger, raising one finger in the air.

"That's right," said Vetch. "Keep it clean!"

Mrs Wilson had wandered over and was listening in to the conversation.

"I feel guilty, you see," said Vetch. "About your conservation area. We all feel guilty."

Kaz and Ginger nodded in agreement.

"And we want to do something about it," continued Vetch. "We've come to offer our help – if you want us, that is."

There was a pause as Tiger and Sam looked towards Mrs Wilson. Kerry's class had just entered the conservation area and she wandered across to join them.

"Well," said Mrs Wilson, scratching her head, "I'm very glad you've, er, seen the light, so to speak. We'd be pleased to accept your help, if you're fit enough, that is! Jump down and join us!"

Vetch, Kaz and Ginger jumped from the wall and joined Mrs Wilson and the children in the conservation area. They were just congratulating each other when a new but familiar sound could be heard approaching the school gate.

"Oh, no – it can't be!" said Sam. "It can't be!"

It was. Scratch came trotting through the gate into the conservation area. His nose was pointing in the air and he was yapping loudly.

"There is such a thing as noise pollution, you know," said Mrs Wilson. "And another thing! I thought you were going to keep that dog on a lead?"

Scratch ambled up to them, the bell on his yellow

collar tinkling away.

"That reminds me," said Vetch, reaching into his pocket. "I've got a present for this animal."

Vetch drew out a smart, brown-leather dog collar and offered it to Tiger.

"I got it from the market. You could say it was on offer."

"Thanks very much," said Tiger, taking the collar and showing it to Scratch. "We'll be pleased to accept. It'll do very nicely when the one he's got now has worn out."

Mrs Wilson smiled and shook her head as Tiger shoved the new collar into his jacket pocket.

"Right," she said. "We've got a lot of work to do if we're going to make our conservation area a success. Let's get on with it, shall we?"